THE CURLY HEAD LETTERS

STORIES TO CURL UP WITH AT CHRISTMAS AND ALL THROUGH THE YEAR

BY GARY LOCKWOOD

To Irene

Stories are never just fiction. They come from memories & dreams. These are my stories. I hope you enjoy them.

Gary Lockwood

TEXT COPYRIGHT 2012 BY GARY LOCKWOOD

ALL RIGHTS RESERVED

TABLE OF CONTENTS

PROLOGUE i

"Christmas Memories" 1

"A Balm in Gilead" 6

"The Sparrow" 12

"The Lullaby" 18

"The Snow Angel" 29

"The Woodcutter" 43

"The Goose" 63

"The Psalm" 73

"The Planter" 83

"Vinnie" 93

"The Beekeeper"..110

"The Grotto"..124

"Buttermilk"...139

"The Creche"..153

"The Curly Head"...166

"The Perfect Tree"..183

"The Codger"...199

"The Cell"...213

"Santa's Moonwalk"...227

"The Rude Elf"...237

"The Postcard"...252

PROLOGUE

I love to write. I learned early the fascination that words have ... how one can roll them around in easy sentences or structure them in elaborate paragraphs in order to evoke not only the simple thoughts conveyed by the letters on the page but also to bring up those deep emotions like laughter and sadness that always linger in the human consciousness.

Many years ago I began to write Christmas stories. I disliked sending the standard holiday card and I also felt that issuing a Christmas letter simply to tell everyone about the events in my family's life was not quite what

I wanted either. I settled on developing an annual Christmas story.

I thought at first that the task would be intimidating and it was at times. I found that my mind refused the work at first and would not concentrate until at least late November when the holiday was already upon the season. Perhaps creativity needed the snow and the cold of winter or the frolic of Christmas lights before it would allow my mind to focus. At any rate, it was always only then, in the week before Christmas, that a kernel of an idea would start to form and my mind would mull it over for a while and finally would take the commission that creativity had offered.

Once I set pen to paper, the task became easier. I was always amazed at how the stories began to flow. It was almost as if the stories were writing themselves. I never knew once I began to write a story how it would end and I was often surprised at the ending. So too was I surprised sometimes at the characters who popped up in the stories . . . characters who in various composite ways had peopled my own life.

The stories were simple at first and neither long nor elaborate. Later, as the characters began to interact and form a community of sorts, the stories became longer and more elaborate. They were, and are, cathartic for me. The writing of them, and now the reading and re-reading of them, releases things inside of me that cannot seem to escape in any other way . . . things like faith, hope, fear, doubt, tears, laughter, and love.

In this book I want to share my stories with you. As you read them, I hope that you will cry with me, laugh with me, and pray with me. Above all, I hope that you will enjoy what I have written.

CHRISTMAS 1992

"CHRISTMAS MEMORIES"

This was my very first attempt at a Christmas story. It was short and sweet but it invoked all the memories of that beautiful time when the warmth of a Christmas morning was still wrapped in the comfortable innocence of childhood. I believe it is a yearning for such innocence that makes us all want to go back home for Christmas year after year.

* * *

It is snowing outside as I write this, covering the ground now with Winter's white blanket. Inside, the fire is crackling and the air is filled with the smell of cookies and pine needles. I am remembering Christmases past when, as a child, I would fall asleep on Christmas Eve "with visions of sugar plums dancing in my head" and would wake on Christmas morning eager with excitement to see if Santa Claus had visited. My parents' home had no central heating in those days and was warmed only by a coal stove which Mom stoked early every morning. Most days the chill in the bedroom was sufficient to keep me cuddled under the quilt for as long as possible but not on that most extraordinary day when the wonders of Christmas were enough warmth for any child.

My folks were not wealthy but somehow they always found the resources to make that morning very special. I would jump from bed and, oblivious to the cold, would dash into the living room to find there the magical yuletide sights and sounds and smells which even now continue to delight my senses as I remember them from so long ago. There were bowls heaped with walnuts and holiday sweets, stockings bulging with chocolates and candy canes, and platters overflowing with cookies and cakes. The scent of nutmeg and cinnamon hung in the air, mixed with that of apples and roast turkey. Softly from the background came the scratchy sound of Silent Night, my mother's favorite song played on the record she liked so much. And always there was the tree, aglow with lights which threw colors of red and yellow, green and blue against the icy masterpiece that Jack Frost had painted on the window.

    I have come to cherish the memories of those early Christmases and of each Christmas since. Like a child, I still delight in the tinsel and the carols. But Christmas is for me today, as an adult, not only a time of great beauty but also of deep meaning and sacred mystery which makes my very soul jump with joy at the fantastic gift which God has given us through the birth of Jesus. It is at Christmas that I remember best my God and His great love and devotion towards His people.

CHRISTMAS 1993

"A BALM IN GILEAD"

Church has always been an important part of my life and I have attended regularly since I was a child. However, I recognize now that for most of my life I was never a true believer. It was only as an adult, during a period of extreme stress, that I suddenly found faith... faith in God and in His son, Jesus Christ my Lord and Savior. That faith has sustained me through many trials and continues to do so.

This story . . . my second . . . is an expression of my faith.

*　*　*

My wife and I are in the city now, having sold our country home last July and moved into a 47th floor apartment in Chicago. From here we have a panoramic view of the skyline and can watch the daily show of city life performed below us. And what a show it is at Christmas! The streets are showered with the soft white glow of Italian lights draped and wreathed about the branches of every conceivable tree.

Here and there along the roadways are tall Christmas trees full of baubles and dressed in radiant colors of red, blue, yellow and green, reflecting their magic against the windows and walls of nearby buildings. There is a Dickensian atmosphere to the town now, a wintery beauty that excites the senses and makes one *experience* Christmas. One can hear Christmas in the shrill cries of vendors hawking roasted chestnuts on State Street and in the clip-clop of hooves as horse carriages move along Michigan Avenue in holiday finery. One can see it in the satisfied smiles of busy shoppers as they rush, packages atilt, towards home and one can see it in the endless twirling energy of the skaters at the Grant Park ice rink. Yes, the city is alive with the pageant of Christmas and we, the spectators, marvel at the enormity of celebration surrounding this anniversary of the Lord's birth. Commercial though it is, secular though it has become, the joyous dance of light and color that is Christmas still proclaims, in a fittingly large, loud, and boisterous manner, Christendom's exultation at the arrival of the Baby King.

    There is profound mystery in Christmas that takes away our very breath and makes tears of overwhelming happiness mixed with contrition well up inside, threatening to burst forth at the approach and touch of God. So much of our lives is spent in the desert, wandering among the sand like the Old Testament people in search of meaning and the Promised Land. Like Jeremiah, we cry out in anguish: "***Is there no balm in Gilead? Is there no doctor there?***" Christmas is God's answer to our plea. Through the birth, life, and death of Jesus, God has taken us out of the desert and into the land that was promised. He has removed the weight of sin from our shoulders and pointed the way to eternal life. What a rich and wonderful gift this is! We are free now to celebrate and to sing loudly the words of the old spiritual: "***There is a balm in Gilead to make the wounded whole. There is a balm in Gilead*** *to heal the sin sick soul*".

CHRISTMAS 1994

"THE SPARROW"

Mornings are always beautiful. Winter mornings are more beautiful than most other mornings. Christmas morning is the most beautiful of all. I wrote the following story on one very early wintery morning in the week before Christmas as I contemplated what wonder the world must have experienced on the dawn of that very first Christmas day.

* * *

Now it is the winter here, the grey season when the world sleeps, covered with memories of summer's warmth and autumn's crisp caress. Still, it is a welcome time for the balmy weather that lasted until but a few days ago precluded thoughts of Christmas. Now, with a chill in the air and Jack Frost chiseling at the window, we can think thoughts of mistletoe and holly, of eggnog and taffy. Even more, we think of holiday hymns and Mary in a manger, cradling the Child King. It was so this morning as I sat by the window preparing to write this letter.

I awoke in darkness and, donning robe, padded barefoot to the breakfast nook to watch the morning chase the night away. On the horizon, across the great lake that laps Chicago's edge, dawn was already painting tiny streaks of crimson and gold in the ink of sky, its brush of wind and cloud dripping splashes of color here and there in the water, there to float in bright patches until, mixed by the waves, they shed their hues into the dark, turning blackness into grey mist.

It had snowed-the first snow of the season-and below in the growing light I could see the city, dressed in white and awaiting the sun like an eager bride awaits her husband's touch. On the sill outside, the snow had banked in a frozen pile against the glass and there in the corner a small sparrow shivered in an igloo depression pecked in the ice, its feathers puffed against the cold. I shivered too, wondering how this small bird could survive such a night of wind and snow.

I thought of another night long ago when a husband and his wife, pregnant with child, had, for want of a room in the inn, shivered in a cave on a Bethlehem hillside, their only companions the beasts of burden and, as I imagine, a small sparrow that had taken refuge there in the hay. How blessed these animals were, for they alone, of all God's creatures on earth, were privileged to see God enter the world in the form of a small baby. Oh how wonderful was that night! The wind still blew.

The cold still numbed the skin. Yet there was a warmth and a peace in that place because God's promise, made through the prophets, was fulfilled:

"Listen! The virgin shall conceive a child! She shall give birth to a Son and He shall be called 'Emmanuel' which means 'God is with us'".

As I watched, the sun melted the clouds and raised its head above the water, spilling liquid light like syrup along the shore where it hardened on frozen ground and exploded into thousands of glittering diamonds scattered over crusted snow. The sparrow raised its head, its breath throwing the first ribbons of morning song into the air. The wind still blew. The cold still numbed the skin. Yet there was warmth and peace. For God is with us.

CHRISTMAS 1995

"THE LULLABY"

My 1995 Christmas story begins with depression. That year was a particularly difficult one for me. My wife and I were empty nesters. We had sold the house in which we had lived for years and in which we had raised our son and daughters. We had left the small comfortable community in which we had both been raised and we had moved into Chicago. It was to have been an adventure for us but events soon began to overtake us, stifling much of the fun we had expected to have. My mother had begun to show obvious signs of Alzheimer's and, as I have since come to learn happens in many families, the siblings, cousins, nieces, nephews, aunts and uncles began to take sides as to what should be done. At the same time, the law firm where I had spent my entire career lost its outward focus and began to struggle mightily with internal issues relating to control, growth and vision for the future. Even my church failed me by forgetting its biblical roots and embarking instead on a walk that seemed to me curiously empty of religious direction. As a result, I often found myself walking aimlessly along streets that seemed empty and cold despite all the bustling activity of the city. It is a frightening thing, I found, to be lonely in the midst of a crowd. This story, called "The Lullaby", depicts some of my struggle. While the story begins with depression, it ends with faith.

* * *

I walked today. It was one of those days in a season of days when there is a lull amid the many parties and gatherings of kin and clan and when the calendar is not chock-a-block with lists of things to do. And so, I walked-partly to declare independence from holiday preparations but mostly to seek the feel of the season, for the Christmas spirit had not yet descended upon me and I hoped that the exercise could thaw the ice inside me which November and December had brought.

I walked west at first, past the towers of Randolph Street, and then I turned north along Michigan Avenue and over the river, its black water throwing steam like chilly wisps of cotton candy into the air as if it was trying to camouflage itself from the huddled buildings that shivered on its banks. Far to the south of the city, as if to avoid it, a frozen sun was setting, its weak light filtering dimly through a thin gauze of grey cloud. The wind was a whip, lashing furiously from the lake and churning frothy waves until they crashed on breakwaters and attacked the shore. Its blows marked my skin with red welts wherever it hit and the sound of its rage had no music within it.

    I could not shake the depression that had settled in my soul and the cold did not help. It is a curious time for a holiday, I thought, when all the warmth of the world has drained away and summer is just another memory locked in ice . . . when all the laughter of the birds is gone and the trees in which they played are just dead sticks, miserable wooden skeletons standing naked beneath a colorless sky.

    Perhaps, I thought, there are cycles of the soul that mirror the seasons of the world. If so, mine was in the deep of winter as if I was lost in the snowy hush of a tangled forest, the dark wood all around hiding the path. It was the same wood where, in the spring of days, before the Serpent whispered in my ear, I had played with Cain and his brother amid the flowers and, giggling like schoolboys in the sunshine, we had chased the thrush from its nest in the wild rose brier and rubbed the golden dandelions against the chin to see who best liked butter. Now, that paradise was lost and the fresh innocence of childhood long ago had given way to the worries, stresses, and sins of the grownups. It was a terrible loss. As I walked, I felt the Old Testament lament of Jeremiah:

"How the gold has grown dim, how the pure gold has changed! The holy stones lie scattered at the head of every street".

Deep in thought, I felt my way further along the Magnificent Mile, oblivious to all except the uneasy feeling within me. At last I came upon the lovely Presbyterian Church, pressed hard against the Watertower area and overlooking the boisterous commotion of the streets below. Despite the din of traffic and the shouts of great hordes of tourists wandering like a gypsy people here to there along the street in search of adventure or treasure, the church rested serenely in its spot, its magnificent circle window painting reflections of cobalt blue, deep scarlet, and pale yellow on the pavement. Something there drew me into the courtyard and bid me rest. I entered and sat for a while on one of the steps. I was about to leave when suddenly from within the quiet building there came the sound of a choir and the sweet voices I heard were like angels calling out for they sang a hymn of great beauty:

"Oh little town of Bethlehem, how still we see thee lie. Above thy deep and dreamless sleep, the silent stars go by. Yet in thy dark streets shineth the everlasting light. The hopes and fears of all the years are met in thee tonight."

It was then, suddenly and mysteriously, that my heart began to warm and I understood anew the magic of Christmas. Perhaps, I thought, it is exactly at this time of year when Christmas must come . . . for it is exactly this time, when the season of the soul has gone into its period of darkness, that God enters with a small candle to forever light the way and makes the great promise that shall never be broken:

"For unto you is born this day in the City of David a Savior who is Christ the Lord."

Oh glorious, lovely, gentle Child who takes away the sins of the world! Oh wonderful, beautiful Baby who reaches out to us and leads us home from the tangled wood!

I sat for a while, listening to the choir. Finally, I stirred. It had become night and as I left the courtyard to return home I saw that the city, its winter coat still muddied and torn, had nonetheless begun to dress for the great celebration, draping itself everywhere with red, green, and white lights like pearls on a string. Everywhere there were wide-eyed children, bundled like tiny Eskimos, their noses pressed excitedly against the shop windows, their breath pasting puffs of crystal frost on the glass. I smiled. For me it was Christmas at last. What a splendid carnival of color and light! The clouds had left now and in the sky a single star shone brightly. Even the wind had calmed and now I could hear its music. It was a lullaby!

CHRISTMAS 1996

"THE SNOW ANGEL"

My father was 41 when I was born. There were other children before me: a brother 18 years my senior and a sister 12 years older. There was also a sister only a year older than I. At some point I learned that there had been a child between the two older siblings, a girl who had died before I was born. It was said that my mother was devastated by the loss and deeply, wildly depressed. Her sadness ended only when my youngest sister was born a year before I was born. It was in that way that my mother and father were parents to two sets of children, separated in age by more than a decade.

While I was still a child I had watched my father grow old. I never felt close to him. I always felt that there was some distance between us ... some wall that I could not climb. I was always jealous of the easy conversation my brother was able to have with my father and I could never fathom why I could not talk to him as easily. Thus it is that one Christmas, shortly before my father died, has extraordinary meaning for me. It was a Christmas when a small event touched him and me in a profound way and allowed us to see into each other's heart for a brief but special moment. I wrote about that moment in my 1996 Christmas story called "The Snow Angel".

* * *

It is late here of a cold December afternoon and I am alone now, resting drowsily in my comfortable corner chair. My wife is out on an important errand and the grandchildren too have gone, leaving only bits of tinseled paper and string here and there on the carpet to remind me that they were here. The loss of their laughter is everywhere and it deepens the silence in the room, making the wind outside seem louder and more insistent as it struggles against the building, trying to get in. On the wall, the shadows dance with the soft Christmas colors flowing from the tree and then, as if frightened, rush away from the harsher reds and oranges thrown through the window by a shivering sun as it reaches low to kiss the earth goodnight and pulls the darkness over its head like a blanket. Sleep approaches. It is the winter twilight, a time for memories and dreams.

It was 1971. My thoughts were to home and to my father for the sickness had come and had already begun to rob him of his vigor. The army had granted leave and so I and my wife had come back home, riding the Silver Zephyr through the bitter night all the way from Kansas with our dog, Pepper, curled at our feet in the tiny compartment and our babies, Jennifer and Lee, asleep in the tiny bed. We had not said much on the journey. Rather, we had held hands in the dark and had talked with our silence.

From Chicago we had continued by car and now, as morning announced our journey's end, we approached the house where I had grown. I was troubled and apprehensive. I remembered my father in his strength. I thought of the night when, with warm, firm embrace, he had held me safe from the lightning storm which so frightened me and, too, the day he had reached down with hard, calloused hands and pulled me piggyback upon his shoulders as he ran along the meadow's edge, darting into the wet coolness of the woods whenever the path allowed and then back again into the tall grass where golden sunlight played among the wildflowers, and we had fallen in a tumble on the ground where I had laughed until my belly hurt. But childhood play had faded and I remembered too the distance that had finally formed between us as I grew older and he had objected to my hair and my clothes and my music. The words had been harsh and then reluctant. It seemed a standoff and we had let the issues fall between us like a wall as I had gone off to college, to marriage and to the army. Now, wiser perhaps, I wished with all my being that I could break through the wall and be again a child so he would hold me against his chest once more and let me listen to the soft, reassuring sound of his heart.

The house was smaller than I remembered and the sugar maples that brooded over the front yard, guarding the way, seemed bigger and darker and more forbidding. Mother, older than before, met us at the door as usual, wearing her apron with the colored pockets and waiving a large mixing spoon. She had been cooking and the sweet smells of Christmas dinner wafted from the kitchen with the promise of turkey and mashed potatoes, cranberries and yams, apple pie and cookies. In the front room, to the children's wonderment, the tree, surrounded by colored packages, was bedecked with candy canes, popcorn strings and circlets made from colored paper. Proudly on top stood the paper angel I had made long ago, faded now and slightly crumpled.

Only my father was missing and I looked around furtively to find him. Mother seemed to read my mind. "He's outside on the roof", she explained. "Why don't you go out and help him?" Her words echoed up from my childhood for I had heard them whenever Father, a true jack-of-all-trades, would retreat to the basement or the garage and I, hopeless mechanic, would be sent to help, there to sit uselessly as my father worked without the need for an apprentice.

I found my father on a ladder, propped up against the house as he chipped away with a small ice pick at the glacier that covered the roof. It seemed an impossible task but I suspected he knew that and had fled to it in order to avoid the conversation our visit entailed. "Mom asked me to help you", I said in greeting, hoping that the starched army uniform with its new sergeant stripes would overcome the unease we both felt.

"Umhm", he grunted, chipping at the ice, and his breath formed a cloud that lingered between us, obscuring his face. I watched his hand dagger at the snow as if in anger.

"Dinner's almost ready", I said. "It smells good". I felt useless. I hoped he wouldn't notice.

"Umhm", he grunted again and chipped harder at the ice.

I began to say something more when I heard it. I sensed the danger in the noise but before I could react, the door pushed open and four year old Jennifer, wrapped like a balloon in pink snowsuit with blue galoshes and scarf, came rushing out, her arms flailing with little girl enthusiasm. Her body rushed headlong into the ladder and I watched in horror as it toppled away from the roof, carrying my father, still clinging to his pick, in an arc through the air to land solidly on his back in the snow.

    I stood aghast, not able to move. Jennifer too seemed a statue as she looked at her grandfather on the ground, her four year old mind recognizing instinctively the result of her negligence. I began to move towards him and, simultaneously, Jennifer's reprimand began to flow from my lips. Suddenly I stopped. My father was smiling. "I'm all right", he said softly. "Don't yell. She's just a baby and I love her. She's your baby and I love you too." Then, as Jennifer pounced laughing on top of him, he began to waive his arms in the snow, making the most beautiful snow angel I had ever seen.

Seeing them, I remembered that day in the meadow and I smiled too.

Later at dinner we read anew the Christmas story. That night there was new meaning in the words. For when I looked across the table at my daughter's eyes I saw my father and I knew that when my father looked at my daughter, he saw me. That day we had closed a distance between us because of a small child. Just so does the Christ Child reconcile the world. Conceived of the Spirit and born of the Virgin, the Christ, fully God and fully man in the mystery of God's plan, brings God and the creation face to face. When we look at the

Christ, we see God. When God looks at the

Christ, He sees us.

CHRISTMAS 1997

"THE WOODCUTTER"

You will see that a recurring theme in my stories is the Woodcutter. He shows up in my stories of Germany and of the farm. Sometimes he is "the hermit" and sometimes he is "the codger". There actually was a woodcutter and I did find him in Germany when my wife and daughter and I lived there during my year at the University of Freiburg. That area of Germany is known for carvers who fashion ornate clocks from the dark wood of the forest that surrounds the town. I found my particular woodcutter one day as I walked through the woods of the famous Black Forest in southwestern Germany. That forest has magnificent, tall trees that grow so closely together that they block the sunlight from the forest floor. The collection of pine needles over eons has padded the forest floor so that it is eerily quiet, making the forest a fairy tale place. No wonder the Brothers Grimm wrote many of their stories in that place. One day, as I walked along through the forest, I came upon a small cottage right in the middle of the wood. The old man who lived there had a full, white beard and long white hair and he was portly. It is not a stretch to say that he looked like Santa Claus. The man was sitting on a chair in the front of his cottage and he was whittling a piece of wood. He was very friendly and I enjoyed a long chat with him. During the whole time, he continued to whittle and I could actually see the form of a deer emerging from the wood.

On one of my many walks through the Black Forest, I also came upon an old graveyard. I have always enjoyed walking through cemeteries and reading headstones. I find the experience both calming to my soul and historically rewarding. In this particular graveyard that day I found a headstone that held a very sad inscription. It was written in

German but the English translation is "She was a rose that the storm broke too early".

In the story that follows, I have melded the two events into one story. It is sad but it reflects my thoughts and feelings during that Christmas season.

One note: I was always reflective about the tragedy that befell Germany during the Hitler years. In my story, the grave of the little girl says she was "getotet" which means she was murdered. The normal word for someone who simply dies would be "gestorben". So the little girl in the story was killed, perhaps during the Nazi years.

A final note: As a child, I always wondered why Santa Claus always gave presents away to children each year. In this story, my woodcutter's name is "Nicholas" and I envisioned him as being Santa Claus, making and giving away toys in honor of his deceased daughter whom he loved so much.

* * *

I looked today at old albums where we keep our precious memories. There among the weddings and birthdays and such I found the pictures of one of our most cherished Christmas holidays. It was Germany in 1968. I had been at college in the United States, studying history and German language and I had been given the chance to study abroad. We'd chosen Albert-Ludwig University in Freiburg im Breisgau, an ancient town nestled deep in Germany's southwest corner and commanding the northern passes through the foothills of the Swiss Alps. Freiburg dated from the 900s and boasted a 10th century cathedral and two stone towers, the Martinstor and the Schwabentor, which had guarded the city gates for over 500 years. A central market square surrounding the cathedral and ringed by medieval buildings now made into hotels and cafes led off into narrow cobblestoned streets that twisted everywhere through the city and turned finally into even narrower pedestrian alleyways filled with quaint little shops where one could buy "echte [genuine]" German things like leder-hosen and cuckoo clocks and marzipan candy. Above the town, brooding and dark, stood the hills of the Black Forest.

We had found a tiny flat near the cathedral and across from the Schwabentor in a building that was itself over 270 years old and, legend has it, had once housed Marie Antoinette. Beneath our window was the "Bach", a rushing mountain stream which tumbled from the hills into a stone channel constructed long ago to follow the mysterious streets of the old city. It was a fairy-book place and in December of that year it was home for me, my wife, and our beautiful baby girl, Jennifer, who was approaching her first birthday.

We had played an awful trick on my in-laws, taking their first and, at the time, only grandchild halfway across the earth. Thus it was that at Christmas they, together with my wife's brother, took their first trip to Europe and came to visit us. We had been preparing for weeks. My wife had made cookies by the dozens and baked apples and sugared candy covered with dollops of chocolate. We had gotten roasted almonds from the grocer and pine boughs and holly from the Sunday morning farmers' market and we had even managed a tiny tree, decorated now with popcorn strings and colored paper and real candles. Topped with the Christmas star, it sat proudly in the window and waited for our guests.

By Christmas Eve morning everything was almost ready. My wife was up early and had set about doing all the final touches. Perhaps in frustration over my lack of initiative in helping her or perhaps in fear that I might pilfer a cookie or knock over a coffee cup, she finally asked me to take Jennifer for a walk in the woods to gather pine cones as a decoration for the table. And so, Jenny, bundled in a parka and stuffed into the backpack like a papoose, and I in my greatcoat with the woolen scarf trundled off into the cold.

It was quiet outside. It had snowed in the night and now a thick wetness covered the world, piled up on the rooftops and the lampposts like pillows. The softness of it muffled the sounds of early morning shoppers as they scurried to finish their holiday tasks and the whiteness of it contrasted with the deep forest green which covered the hills. As I walked, the Christmas chimes of the cathedral began to play. The music mixed with the winter wind and flew away.

We took the sky-tram up the side of the "Hochberg", the high hill which overlooked the town. From the top one could see southward over the valley all the way to Switzerland and France. In the 1500s there had been a great battle on the hill and the huge cannons and cannonballs were still in place, preserved now in a park that the citizens used for summer picnics and as a starting point for walks in the deep woods. There were only a few there today and those that were huddled close to the tram entrance as if fearing they would lose return privileges if they moved away.

The snow had not reached the mountain and the paths into the woods were clear, covered only by the thick padding of pine needles that had collected over a thousand years. We selected one which followed the hillside at first and then cut through an open meadow and finally enveloped us in the stillness of the forest.

It was eerie there and a bit magical. There was little underbrush for the life giving sun rarely penetrated the thick canopy of the trees. In winter, the clouds hung low over the branches, casting dark misty shadows and painting the forest with shades of grey and black.

Jenny and I enjoyed our walk. I stooped now and then to gather pine cones, stuffing them like boyhood treasures into the oversized pockets of my coat. Once we saw a rabbit which quickly fled into the dark. At length we came to a clearing in the midst of which sat a tiny cottage painted white and blue and bedecked with ornamental flourishes as if a woodcarver had devoted a lifetime there. Outside, on a tiny bench, sat an old man, his wrinkled face almost totally obscured by a head of silky white hair flowing to his shoulders and a white beard which billowed down to his belt. I could see only his bulbous nose which had reddened in the cold and his deep blue eyes which twinkled in greeting like patches of sunlight on the water.

"Guten Tag", he said and the friendliness of his tone drew me closer. He was hunched over, working something with his hands.

"Guten Tag", I replied. I could see that he had been whittling a small block of wood. As I watched he continued to work, flicking his knife quickly over the wood as tiny chips flew here and there in the air.

"Wie alt ist das Baby [How old is the baby]?", he asked, pointing at Jennifer. As he spoke he raised his hand to his ear and wiggled the lobe of it at Jenny, chuckling as he did. Then he went back to his task, turning the wood over and over in his hands as he chipped away.

"Ein Jahr [one year]", I said. It was a reindeer! I could see clearly now the shape of the horns and the legs as they began to climb from the block of wood. He continued to work, polishing and shaping and smoothing until the deer seemed alive.

He must have seen my excitement for he held the tiny animal up for me to see. "Ein Geshenk fur meine Tochter [a gift for my daughter]", he said. "Morgan is ihre Geburtstag [tomorrow is her birthday]." He hesitated then and, looking at Jenny cuddled deep in the backpack, he turned and offered the toy to me. "Gib's dem Baby [give it to the baby]", he said.

"Nein", I exclaimed. "Es gehort Irer Tochter [it belongs to your daughter]".

"Kom", he said. "Folgst du mir [follow me]". With that, he stood and walked quickly behind the cottage. Jenny and I followed. There, flush upon the forest and hidden by a small grove of trees was a tiny cemetery, its well-kept graves and markers surrounded by a white picket fence. The old man opened the gate and went inside with Jenny and me close behind.

"Meine Tochter [my daughter]", he said, pointing to one of the graves. The stone read: "Greta Muller, Tochter von Greta und Nicholaus Muller, geboren 25 December 1922- getotet 2 Mai 1935". Further down the stone read: "Sie war eine Rose die der Sturm zu fruh gebrochen hat [she was a rose that the storm broke too early]".

I said nothing. I looked in his eyes and saw the sudden sadness there mixed with the twinkle. It was quiet, the only sound a bird somewhere in the forest. From far below I could hear the bells of the cathedral. "Gib's dem Baby", he said again. "Greta is mit Jesu im Himmell. Das Leben und das Lieben sind jetzt am wichtigsten. Dieses Baby ist jetzt meine Tochter. Du bist mein Sohn [Greta is in heaven with Jesus. Life and love are now the most important things. This baby is my daughter now and you are my son]". And then he smiled and, pressing the tiny reindeer into my hand, he turned, went out the gate, and disappeared into the forest.

That night, Mom and Dad, my wife, her brother, our daughter and I celebrated Christmas Eve. At midnight we took the tiny tree outside on the footbridge over the Bach and lit the candles. As the flames burned brightly in the night and we sang our Christmas hymns, I thought of a little girl named Greta who had burned brightly for a little over 12 years and then had fallen in the storm of life. I thought, too, of another child – the Christ child – who had come that Christmas day so long ago so that He might calm the storm. I knew that the old woodcutter was right. Greta was in heaven with Jesus. She had been a gift from God just as every child is a gift. I knew that the man could never stop loving Greta and yet he had learned that love cannot be locked away in the heart for it turns bitter there. Its sweetness only survives if it is given away. I fingered the tiny reindeer in my pocket, my daughter's first Christmas gift, and knew that it had been a gift of love from the old woodcutter named

Nicholas, his only way to tell his daughter how much he still loved her.

CHRISTMAS 1998

"THE GOOSE"

Fascinating to me is that in some cases the memory can bring to life not only the particular sights of an event long past but also the precise smells and the exact sounds that accompanied the event. My story of "The Goose" is an attempt to describe one such event which is marked in my memory. I don't know why this specific memory is so strong but it rests there in my mind in vivid color and full detail. I still know today, more than half a century later, the exact location of the farmhouse where my father collected the goose. I can actually still smell the tobacco smoke and dust that saturated the cushioning of the old car and I can still hear the music that came from that old radio. Most of all, I remember the closeness I felt for my father that particular night. Please enjoy my story of "The Goose".

*　*　*

There is a Peace in Christmas that calms me and, like a sweet lullaby, whispers quiet amid the raging storms of life. Perhaps it is the simple beauty of it that counsels silence over the world's unending noise . . . a million and more lights of every color shining comfort from the dark like candles on a giant cake. Perhaps it is the music of it . . . a melody of angel voices throwing songs in the air to float softly on the winter winds. Perhaps it is the smell of it . . . evergreen mixed with candles and the scent of cookies and pie wafting from the kitchen. Most of all, I think, it is the message of Christmas that holds me close like a baby to its mother and kisses tears from my eyes: For God loved the world so much that He sent His only Son that whoever believes in Him shall not perish but shall have eternal life. Hallelujah!

There was a Christmas long ago when the Peace touched me. I was ten that year, just a wisp of a boy. My father worked a factory day shift then and the week before Christmas each year the factory gave every worker a turkey. That year the business had been very profitable and each employee received a cash bonus in addition to the turkey. In celebration, my parents allowed that part of the money should go to prepare a splendid Christmas dinner for family and other friends. It was decided there should be a goose in addition to the turkey and so my father called about to find a fresh one. He knew a farmer who raised geese and, contacting him, my father quickly closed the deal . . . two dollars for a freshly slaughtered goose but father would have to pick it up, pluck it, and dress it for the dinner.

Late that afternoon my father prepared to collect the goose. To his chagrin, my mother, at the last moment, wondered aloud whether he wanted me along "to help". Without waiting for an answer, I grabbed my coat and quickly installed myself in the front seat of the old Studebaker that he had left warming up in the garage. With a muted "harrumph" and a last glance at my mother, my father moved behind the wheel, gunned the car backward up the inclined driveway to the street, forced the gearshift into the drive position, and off we went.

What had once been plush brown carpet covering the seats in the old car was now ragged and worn and smelled of tobacco smoke and dust. Still, the seats were comfortable and I settled back, listening to the static of voices as father turned the radio dials. The sun hung low in the sky like a frozen orange and as it sank below the horizon, the darkness rushed from the woods to surround us. The headlights of the car fought back, throwing spears of dim yellow light onto the road to allow passage. The night was cold and it quickly hardened the snow that crunched like broken crystal beneath the tires.

The car turned at last onto a rutted dirt path that wound its way carefully through the trees and stopped finally by an old farmhouse where a Christmas tree totally bedecked with blue lights stared from the window. "Stay here", my father said, cutting the engine and pointedly pocketing the keys as if he expected I might otherwise try to drive home without him. I didn't stay. As soon as my father was in the house, I left the car and walked toward the old barn where I had seen the deer disappear.

    A full moon had risen and now it poked its silvery head over the monster oaks behind me and threw frozen blue shadows into the snow. Like a river, the moonlight flowed around the barn and flooded the pasture beyond. The buck, with a doe at its side, stood there, its great horns held high like huge candlesticks. Along the fence a dog crept slowly on crusted snow towards a tiny bush that had pushed its way out of the drifts.

As I watched, the dog became a fox and the bush turned suddenly into a shivering little rabbit, unsure of its escape. I pushed close to the barn, hoping to blend with the wood . . . fascinated by the saga of life and death playing out before me . . . fearful to move lest the buck bolt for the forest on the far side.

The fox crept closer and closer to the rabbit, its breath exploding now and then with tiny bubbles of steam. The rabbit kept its position as if it was already dead. Suddenly, the buck turned and stepped slowly towards the barn. The doe did the same and the rabbit, perhaps seeing its chance, rushed between them. The fox too turned until I could see the yellow shine of its eyes. All four animals stopped then and stared in my direction.

    I did not hear my father until he was there beside me. "They're looking at the Christmas star", he said in a whisper, his head nodding briefly upward towards the sky. I looked up to see a brilliant star floating next to the moon as if the two were engaged in a dance of light. When I looked back the animals were moving away . . . the fox in one direction, the rabbit in another and the two deer in a third. "Merry Christmas, son", my father said, handing me the goose.

I do not know what planet it was that night . . . whether Jupiter or Saturn or Venus. For me, it was and always will be the Christmas star. My father and I rode home that night and we actually talked . . . about deer and foxes and rabbits and geese . . . and he told me about the prophecy he had read somewhere: **The wolf shall dwell with the lamb, and the leopard shall lie down with the kid, and the calf and the lion and the fatling together, and a little child shall lead them.**

CHRISTMAS 1999

"THE PSALM"

My mother was a big influence in my life. Like my father, she was born shortly after the 19th century ended and the 20th century began. Her life began at a time when most people in the United States lived on small farms in rural landscapes, before industrialization and invention changed the time parameters within which people moved and lived. It was a simpler time and, given the stresses and strains of modern life, an inviting one. I was always amazed at the stories she could tell … of a time before cars, before airplanes, before television … many of them gleaned from her own parents who lived through much of the latter part of the 19th century. I see her stories in my own musings as I tell my children and grandchildren about my childhood when there were no interstate highways, no cell phones, no computers. The stories give a sense of the passage of time and of history and of generational change as they flow from one century to the next and again into the next. So too flowed not only the stories of life but also the stories of faith practiced over the years. My mother died in 1999 and that year I wrote this Christmas story as a tribute to her.

* * *

"***<u>The Lord is my shepherd. I shall not want.</u>***"

The old woman sat sleeping in her favorite chair, her head slumped down against her chest and her body wrapped in a knit shawl which she grasped with gnarled fingers and held tightly against her throat despite the warmth pouring through the window from the afternoon sun. On the wall above the woman hung The Twenty-Third Psalm, stitched in red letters on faded white cotton and framed with simple strips of wood painted black.

There was nothing obvious to associate the sewing with the woman but I knew she had made it. The psalm was a favorite . . . underlined in the big bible which she had kept in the bed stand . . . and from my childhood I remembered the stitching that had always hung above the sink in the kitchen. The woman was fragile now . . . her mind almost silenced by the Alzheimer's, her hands twisted with arthritis and age. Speech eluded her now and her eyes did not work well. Still, she knew that she wanted to be there . . . in the favorite chair . . . under the words of the psalm.

"***He makes me lie down in green pastures. He leads me beside still waters. He restores my soul.***"

For her, there were meanings in the words. The woman had come from farm folk ... 14 children and she, at 90, the last. She was of the country ... she had known it and all its quiet ways ... had known, too, the green places and the secret places where cool, clear water sprang from the ground and bubbled through the rocks to collect finally in the meadow pond where of an early morning the deer would come to drink. There was beauty there and peace which whispered comfort to her soul and so she had kept the places in her heart just as she kept the psalm and its meanings.

"<u>He leads me in the paths of righteousness for His Name's sake.</u>"

The lines in the woman's face told of troubles... of prayers denied and dusty dreams laid aside. She had buried a husband and two children. Still, she had kept the meanings. Once as a schoolboy, I and my chums had learned that little disks punched from sheet metal in shop class worked as nickels in the telephones. Caught and confronted, I tried to explain that the others had pressured me and left me no choice in the scheme. The woman wanted nothing of it. "There is always a choice", she had thundered, "and it's you doin' the choosin'" Her tears and my shame mingled that day and taught a lesson about the pathways of life.

"**<u>Yea, though I walk through the valley of the shadow of death, I shall fear no evil. For You are with me. Your rod and Your staff, they comfort me.</u>**"

One December morning she came early and jostled me to wake. "Come see God's Christmas tree", she whispered and led me barefoot to the porch. There was mist on the field that day. It had rolled from the river in the night as the air had warmed. In the dark, it had crept unobserved through the rows of corn stubble which lined the hill and in the hours before the dawn it had slid down into the meadow which bordered the great woods. Now, as morning began to paint the sky, it lay upon the earth like a huge blanket of cotton candy stretching over the entire valley.

"There", she said, pointing her finger at the middle of the great grounded cloud. "There is God's tree!" I saw it then . . . the huge pine tree which always stood sentinel in the pasture, its trunk and uppermost branches poking now through the mist. Its bottom hidden in the fog, the part that I could see floated on the cloud, its size and shape the perfect Christmas tree. As we watched, the sun began to decorate the tree with the morning, throwing reds and oranges and yellows onto the branches.

"It's beautiful!", she exclaimed and as she spoke I saw the same beauty reflected in her eyes. "Do you know why the evergreen is the symbol of Christmas?", she asked. My silence prompted an answer. "Because the evergreen never dies."

"***You prepare a table before me in the presence of my enemies. You anoint my head with oil. My cup runs over. Surely goodness and mercy shall follow me all the days of my***

life and I shall dwell in the house of the Lord forever."

"Because the evergreen never dies", she had said and in the words was her faith ... a simple faith born of the country and stitched into the psalm. I watched her now as she slept in the chair and as the day faded outside the window. I knew that she would dwell in the house of the Lord forever.

CHRISTMAS 2000

"THE PLANTER"

I have always loved farms. My father's people were all farmers, having come to McHenry County, Illinois shortly after it was opened to white settlement and established themselves along the Fox River south of the town of McHenry. My father was born there on a farm that still stands today. Although I grew up in town, I spent some of my childhood summers at my uncle's farm in Crystal Lake, Illinois. Many of the characters in my stories are based on the people I met there during those idyllic days.

* * *

He was a planter. All his life he had worked the soil . . . reasoning with it, cussing it, cajoling it, digging it with gnarled fingers as hard and twisted as hickory wood. His people had come from Pennsylvania and had settled early in the county where they had worked the rich bottomlands along the Fox River, their toil each year producing a bounty of corn and squash and pumpkins and potatoes. He had worked with them. He had worked in the dry and the wet. He had worked in the cold and the heat ... and he had sacrificed. Once, because he'd not paid attention, the corn god demanded a finger, using the husker to rip it from him. Yes, he had worked and toiled and sacrificed and his sweat had baptized the ground and blessed it ... watering it so it would yield. He was a planter and in the planting was his being. In the planting was his soul.

I think it was this had made him so stubborn that year when the woman asked to cut the tree. It were a perfect shape, she argued, and if he could cut just right, 'twould nicely fit the spot in the parlor where folks would see in the window as they got to the house from the drive. After all, trees were dear expensive in town, she said, and the trouble to get one, well, that were silly when their own, home-grown, were for the taking.

But he wanted none of it and refused. After all, it was he had planted the tree . . . one of the seedlings got from the church at $5 the bunch. Most had died but this, atop the hill above the pond, had prospered tall and thick, its brooding, evergreen branches forming the dark, secret places where the birds would hide the night as the storm winds screamed only to emerge at dawn to bless the morning calm with song.

We could see the tree from the kitchen . . . a sturdy sentinel to mark the seasons year by year. In spring, the melt receded beneath the tree . . . a dark and muddy patch quickly filled with crocuses, daffodils, and tulips sprung from the bulbs he had gently laid there . . . these to dance in the early winds until the summer grasses –junegrass and bottlebrush and, closer on the pond, big bluestem-overtook and surrounded. There the butterflies played in the sunlight and matched their colors with the pink of the cornflowers and the purple of the milkweed and the deep scarlet of the leadplants. There, in fall, the deer gathered before their trek to the deep woods to winter. There, when

December snow began to fall, the tree gathered it like a blanket and went to sleep, waking now and then to whisper comfort to the farm and promise warmth's return.

"No", the planter in him said. "I won't cut that tree."

They had argued then and when the words were through, he donned his coat and sloshed out into the snow towards the barn. Seeing him go, the woman retreated to the parlor where she looked at the spot and glanced wistfully through the window at the drive. She opened the old phonograph and chose a record of Christmas music. Returning to the kitchen, she looked at me. "He's gone to be with the rest of the mules", she said. Then she turned her efforts to the supper.

    It's hard to remember now how long he was out there that night or where he got what he needed or whether the cows got milked although I suspect they did. What I remember is that from the kitchen window I watched him time to time come out of the barn and trudge up the hill into the dark towards that tree as if to visit it and pass on some thought had come to him during the chores or to discuss some fine point which needed clarification in the negotiations. Each time he vanished in the night I saw him re-appear some bit later in the circle of frozen light thrown by the naked bulb hung over the barn door. Back and forth he went and I watched him intently just as the woman ignored him with one eye and continued to fuss with the cooking of the meal.

Finally, he reentered the kitchen and placed his coat, steaming in the warmth, on the hook by the door. The woman turned, holding a spoon in the air like a wand as if to turn him into a frog and I could see in her eyes that she was trying to decide whether to actually feed him the meal.

He spoke first. "Merry Christmas", he said and he flipped the switch by the door. Outside, the tree exploded with the glow of a hundred and more colored bulbs, their gentle lights dripping through the green boughs and falling like watercolors in the snow, pooling there and running slowly downhill to the pond where they slid on the ice and formed a second tree, as beautiful as the first.

    We stood at the window for a long time and watched the lights as they floated in the night. A soft snow began to fall. From the parlor came the scratchy strains of "Silent Night" and we sang along. Finally the woman looked to him and took his hand. "Let's eat", she said.

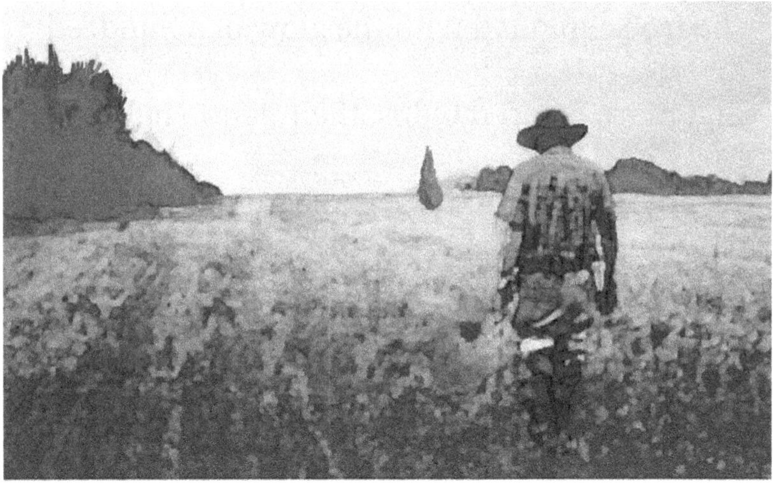

CHRISTMAS 2001

"VINNIE"

My family has a military history. Ancestors on my father's side fought at the Battle of Bunker Hill and in the Civil War. My mother's brother, Ralph, saw major combat in France during World War I (we still have handwritten letters he wrote from the battlefield). Many of my cousins fought in World War II. My brother fought in Korea. I served in the Army during the Vietnamese War.

Yet despite the military thread that runs through my family's history, there has always been recognition of the trials of war and a profound understanding of the miseries, the ugliness, and the atrocities of war. In the stories my family told, there was always an acknowledgement that war is not to be desired but rather, feared and avoided if at all possible. The stories also told of the disruption and heartbreak that visited the home front whenever war caused the separation and dislocation of spouses, of lovers, of mothers and sons.

Stories of the home front were part of my childhood. I was born in 1946, about sixteen months after the end of World War II. The tales of the conflagration the world had just gone through in the years before my birth were fresh and vivid. They were told regularly and they were often infused with poignancy, not the least because my mother's family was German. Although they had migrated here in the latter part of the 19th century and had established themselves as successful farmers on the rich prairies of northern Illinois and southern Wisconsin, a full 70 years or so of life in the United States had not fully extinguished the language and traditions of the old country. My grandmother and grandfather still spoke the guttural "plattdeutsch", or low German, at home. Although several of their sons had fought the Germans in the first Great War and many grandsons and granddaughters served in the U.S. military during the Second World War, the supposed "taint" of being German still affected my grandparents greatly. They spoke in whispers of how they fearfully huddled in the darkness the night certain townspeople had appeared outside their house and had thrown a brick through their window, shouting "krauts go home". My aunt told the story of how she had sewn an American flag onto her dress only to have it ripped away by other children who said she was not an American.

On September 11, 2001, the United States went to war again after hate-filled religious fanatics decided that their god would approve the destruction of thousands of innocent lives and appointed themselves as the instrument of that destruction. Everyone alive on that day and old enough to appreciate the meaning of the event knew that their world had been profoundly changed. As I wrote my Christmas story that year, I reflected on the war we had just entered and I wondered how our lives would change in the months and years to come. My story tries to weave together the two emotions I had at the time, emotions gleaned no doubt from the earlier stories my family told.

First, I had a great pride in the military capability of the United States and the role that citizen soldiers play in the military. Second, I feared the darkness and turmoil I knew the war would bring. My story revolves around Vinnie, a composite character fashioned from many boys I knew in childhood, and how his military service in time of war affected the neighborhood he left behind. The story is titled simply "Vinnie".

* * *

Vinnie Pisciotti was my hero. The only Italian kid in a neighborhood of English, Irish, and German names, he was a Chicago lad come to live among the country boys. Despite his city background-or perhaps because of it-Vinnie could do everything. He could climb a tree faster and higher than the rest of us. He could hurl a jackknife at the porch rail and stick it far into the wood. He could hit a baseball a mile and do it from the left or the right. Vinnie was afraid of nothing and of no one and he always made the rest of us feel courageous too.

    Three years older than I, Vinnie looked after me like I was a younger brother. He taught me how to whistle and how to throw a curve ball. He taught me how to aim a slingshot and where to find just the right size skipping stones to fling across the pond behind McDuff's barn. That night on the basketball bus when the older boys had made fun, he sat with me and talked the whole ride to let them know that he was my friend and I, his. Once, at his uncle's farm, he had rushed to the rescue and fought off the pig with a stick after I was foolish enough to fall head first into the pen.

When he was old enough to use his papa's rifle, we often walked deep into the big woods to hunt rabbits and squirrels. Vinnie was good at it. He knew all the trails and how to tell directions from the moss and where to find walnuts and how to strip the shagbark from the hickories in order to make a fine fire. He seemed to know what the wind whispered as it moved through the forest and whether it foretold storms or not and he knew the meaning of all the bird sounds. He shared with me the secret clearing near the hill where the cave cut sideways into the sandstone and water bubbled from the rock and it was there that we often camped and hid ourselves from the world as we cooked the bounty of our hunt and told stories and romanced about pirates and cowboys. Vinnie was my hero. He could do everything.

It was no surprise that Vinnie joined the army after high school. After all, his papa was a war hero who had fought and died at a place called Iwo Jima. Vinnie became what the army called a "ranger" and we were all so proud when he came home after training. Mrs. Pisciotti made a party and invited the whole neighborhood and Vinnie wore his uniform and showed us the funny little green beret that went with it. He showed us his orders too and told us about a place called Vietnam which no one had heard of and we all remarked on it and pulled out a map to see where it was. When Vinnie left, we were all sad.

For months, Mrs. Pisciotti kept us all posted and she would bring around the letters from Vinnie and we would read about the heat and the jungle and the lushness and the beauty and the greenness of the place. He never mentioned exactly where he was except to talk about the "highlands" as if that should make it crystal clear for all of us. Instead, we read the names in the newspapers and learned of distant places like Pleiku, Dong Hoi, Da Nang, China Beach and Saigon. After a while, the tone of his letters changed and he wrote of the drudgery and the fatigue and sometimes of the battles. Each night on the television we saw the helicopters and the bombs and the blood and we went to bed and we shuddered in the dark for Vinnie and for ourselves.

    It was around June when the letters stopped coming and shortly after that when Mrs. Pisciotti stopped visiting. We would still see her on her way to town or walking in her garden and we would visit her from time to time but it was not the same as before for her beauty had aged and seemed brittle and her smile looked frozen as if it had been pasted on her face to hide something too terrible to reveal. There was no official word, of course, but the telephone call had said "missing" and the neighbors whispered worse. As summer faded into autumn and autumn disappeared beneath winter's snow, we ceased to whisper and we began to mourn.

On Christmas Eve day it began to snow hard and the wind blew itself into a blizzard and the cold marched down from the north, flinging ice on the trees and crusting the ground wherever it went. In such a storm there could be no thought of travel and so plans were canceled, leaving pastries and cookies to go wasting. It was my father who thought of Mrs. Pisciotti then and, donning parkas and gloves and galoshes, we gathered up two pies-the cherry and the pumpkin-and made the perilous trek across the road to wish her a Merry Christmas.

Her house was mostly dark as we approached, the only light coming from the small Christmas tree in the parlor. Her door was open and we went in. We found Mrs. Pisciotti hunched in the cushioned chair by the fireplace, tears streaming on her face and a paper clutched in her hand. Her sobs drowned the holiday music from the record player in the corner. I looked at her and at my father. The pies seemed heavy as lead and I feared they would fall to the floor before I found a place to rest them. Putting one carefully on the mantle, I reached for the paper in her hand. It was a telegram. I began to read, hesitantly at first and then, as I began to understand, I read more quickly, the most important words jumping out at me like firecrackers:

"HAPPY ... REPORT ... YOUR SON ... SPECIALIST 4, VINCENT J. PISCIOTTI, NOW

SAFE . . . WOUNDED . . . DA NANG HARBOR . . . TRANSFER WEST GERMANY . . . HOSPITAL . . . ."

The other pie fell from my hands and spattered on the rug but it did not matter. I let out a war whoop which startled and confused my father until he too had seen and read the telegram. I could see now that Mrs. Pisciotti's tears were tears of joy. Reaching down, I pulled her from the chair and together we danced a jig across the room.

That night we stayed at Mrs. Pisciotti's until late in the evening. My father called all the neighbors and one by one they found their way through the storm, carrying cards and gifts and cakes and cookies and plants. The snow continued to fall outside and the cold hammered against the doors and the window panes. But inside the fire blazed, the tree glistened, candles flamed on the mantle, we sang songs and told stories and Mrs. Pisciotti again brought out Vinnie's letters and showed them to everyone. It was one of the best Christmas parties ever.

One night, after Vinnie returned, he and I went walking again in the big woods, following the trails we had known before when the world was still a child. The night was clear and cold and the moon scattered its light like diamonds across the crusted snow. As we walked, a rabbit fled from the trees and across our path. "How about a hunt?" I asked.

Vinnie stopped for a long time and looked up at the stars. Finally, he reached down, took a handful of snow, and licked it into his mouth. "No", he said. "I don't hunt anymore".

CHRISTMAS 2002

"THE BEEKEEPER"

There is such controversy today about so-called "illegal immigration". I have mixed feelings about it. On the one hand, being a lawyer, I believe we must be a nation of laws and that anarchy results when laws are ignored. On the other hand, I know that people have been arriving in this country unannounced for centuries and for much of that time there were no laws to prevent the movement of people who desired to come here. The story is that my own grandfather came to this country in about 1873, ostensibly to visit his own parents who had come here from Germany in the 1860s, but in reality to avoid the mandatory military service in Prussia. He stayed and never went back. At some point he was granted citizenship here in the United States.

My Christmas story for 2002 tells about a Mexican, probably an illegal worker, who showed up each spring on my uncle's farm to help with the work through the summer. The man was a simple man with an encyclopedic knowledge of forest plants, both edible and medicinal. He was also a keeper of bees and he seemed to know everything about them. An interesting fact about the man was that he was deathly allergic to bee stings and would puff up like a balloon if one stung him. They rarely did although I would see him many times with hundreds of bees covering his hands and arms as he worked with them. At any rate, this man took a liking to me and I to him. He taught me many things about the forest and about plants and about bees. He also taught me things about people, especially how to treat them, illegal or not.

* * *

  The old man loved bees. He would arrive by the farm in the early season, looking always the tramp as he trudged the muddy footpath that followed the creek in its rush from the hills, a towel, like a babushka, twined tightly on a stick to hold his treasures. No one seemed to know, or care, where he went in winter. "South" was all they would say. But his appearance each year at the beginning of spring always meant an end to the cold and a return of warm winds brushing north over frozen fields, sweeping the snow into piles that turned finally into small pools of melt water, and painting the land with pastels of every imaginable hue. "I follow the winds", the old man said, "because they wake the bees from sleep".

The farmer would greet him fondly each year not only because there was much to do about the place when he arrived what with the planting chores and the need to clean the barn when the cows were put to pasture again, but also because the farmer missed the old man in the idle months when the dark and the cold smothered the farmer's soul and forced him inside to contend with the sullenness of the woman. "How are you, Jose?", the farmer would ask and the two would shake hands and hug and the farmer would uncork some of the hard cider and they would toast to health and talk about the weather and the crops and the animals and they would boast about who would win at the pinochle.

    The woman was not as kind. She always called the old man "that Mexican" and made clear he was not welcome in "her house" but would needs make do with sleeping in the little room the farmer had cobbled together in the barn loft with plywood and planks, packing the spaces between with paper and burlap. The old man had finished the job with hay bales stacked against the outside walls to insulate the room and inside he laid the floor with quilts and blankets for bedding, another bale for a chair, and a small lamp that, with the help of many cords snaking through the barn, plugged into the farm's electricity and threw enough yellow light into the room to make it just comfortable.

    The old man always called me "'migo poco" and let me go about with him as he tended chores and, after the work, when he wandered the pasture and the woods. He knew the land, this old man. He knew its secrets . . . knew its hidden things . . . and as we walked he would teach me the wonders, as if he were a father instructing a son. There, in a process he called "the collecting", he would gather things like a shopper in a grocery store. There was chicory to cut for coffee and there were dandelions to make the sweet, syrupy wine that he and the farmer would drink on hot summer evenings as they sat on the bench by the hollyhocks just out of sight of the woman. By the barren tree in the meadow grew the gooseberry bushes which yielded soft, green balls of fruit as small as marbles and sour as a lemon drop. At the pasture's edge, where the trees began to fight the sunlight, he would find mulberries and raspberries and, further in, where the brambles locked arms to prevent passage, were the blackberries, dangling in the thicket like ornaments on a tree. In the wet by the creek he would pluck sticky resin from the underleaf of some silvery plant and we would chew it like gum, its licorice flavor tingling on the tongue.

He knew the wildflowers, too. There were buttercups on the hillside and noonflowers in the lawn, their silly heads asleep in the grass by mid-morning. In the field were white daisies and purple thistles growing thick and everywhere was Queen Anne's Lace, its dainty doily flowers spoiled by the tiny pinprick of blood red in the center. By the fence grew black-eyed-susans and in the shadow of the oaks was the briar rose bush where the thrush kept its nest. The old man loved the flowers and at times he would pick some to brighten his room. Most, however, he left for the bees.

The old man knew bees the best. The farmer said the old man had found the colony by following a wild beeline into the woods until he found the honey tree. Then he built the hive and brought the queen back to it by smoking the nest to find her. The rest of the bees followed and they stayed. The old man and I would often sit in the hickory grove near the hive, our backs to the trees, to watch the bees work. The old man would say which were the drones and which the soldiers and they would gather on his hands and arms, never stinging for they seemed to know he was friend. We would watch their travel each day as they flew out in a frantic search for nectar and the old man would know from the direction and the timing which flowers the bees had visited and how the honey might taste because of it. First thing each year when he arrived, the old man would visit the hive, remove the screen containing the honeycomb, and pick the dead workers from the cluster of half dormant bees. "They surround the queen to protect her . . . to keep her warm", he explained. "She lives but some of them die".

It was September when it happened. The leaves of the hardwoods had already turned and begun to fall and the old man should have been gone yet wasn't. Autumn rains had stopped the cutting and he had stayed to help the harvest. It was the woman who caused it. It was she who threw the rake in pique at the footprints on the kitchen floor, screaming at the old man as to how wronged she'd been by him having stepped foot in the kitchen at all. It was she who missed, hitting the hive instead. The bees swarmed then at the disturbance and she could not outrun them. Flailing, twisting, and shouting, the woman fell to the ground as the bees swirled above like dive bombers on the attack. It was the old man who saved her. Seeing her fall, he threw his jacket over her face and laid his body atop hers, shielding her from the wrath of the bees that poured their venom into him instead.

It was odd after that. The old man was rushed to hospital and never returned to the farm that year. As fall froze and turned to winter, the farmer moved inside and sat with the woman in silence, speaking little about anything and even less about what had happened with the bees. They never said what had become of the old man and I wondered if he, like the bees he loved so much, had died saving the queen. It was only later, when the box arrived, that I knew the old man was alright. It had been sent from Mexico and the note was written to "'migo poco" and it said "Felice Navidad". Inside the box, tied with a red ribbon, was a jar of honey.

CHRISTMAS 2003

"THE GROTTO"

There is a grotto. It is a magical place in the middle of a forest near LaCrosse, Wisconsin on land my in-laws once owned. I remember how fascinated I was on the day I found the grotto. It was a concave-shaped sandstone cliff that rose from the otherwise flat forest floor. A shallow depression of the ground at the foot of the cliff had filled with water and from the tracks left in the mud it was obvious that deer and other animals came there often to drink. I always wanted to climb the cliff but I never did. In this story, called "The Grotto", my imagination allowed me to finally reach the top.

* * *

It was late afternoon on a sweltering August day when we found the tree. It was Vinnie found it first actually and ran to the field to tell the bunch of us, interrupting the haying as he came. "It's the perfect shape", he said excitedly. "It's just the gettin'll be hard."

Vinnie's discovery gave us all an excuse to quit the chores. Like schoolchildren released early from class, we let out a loud "whoop" and then Vinnie and I, Jeff the hired hand, and the young twins all piled into the farmer's truck, throwing out a few of the bales to make room. Vinnie drove, racing the old vehicle across the pasture and scaring the cows as he went. Shirtless and tired, the rest of us laughed as we bumped along and felt the cooling touch of the wind as it dried the sweat from our skin. On the far side, Vinnie turned the truck onto the rutted dirt path that led to the big woods.

It was cooler under the trees and after a while the boys and I put our shirts back on. The hired hand usually had a long-sleeved flannel shirt, even on the hottest of days. He put his on now and sat with his back against the tailgate in the rear of the pickup, his eyes closed and his shirt buttoned at the neck, enveloping him like a cocoon.

The trail led up along the side of the hill until it reached the top and then it flattened out and wandered along the ridges that connected hill to hill. Now and then the road would dip between the hills and Vinnie would have to brake as we went down and then gun the old machine hard as we climbed again. At times the road became little more than a footpath and once or twice it seemed to be just a parting in the thicket as ferns, small saplings and other dense undergrowth fought for position. Vinnie seemed to know exactly where to go for he seldom hesitated. At last he slowed the truck and then stopped altogether.

Vinnie was right. The tree would be hard to get. The place was far off the road and required us to leave the truck and walk a distance through thick underbrush. The evergreen was growing atop a ledge in the face of the rock near but not quite at the top of a curved sandstone formation which rose cliff-like from the forest floor and served as the single wall to an area we called the "grotto" because it cut deep into the rock like a small cave. The floor of the grotto collected rainwater, making the ground there wet and swampy so that the only approach was muddy and difficult. More unfortunate than that, the grotto where the tree was growing was in the no-man's land between the farmer's property and the McDuff's farm. No one knew who owned the land there for the memory of it was lost or, worse, had changed according to the telling of the story and who was doing the telling. Both men claimed the land but neither could prove the right so at last the land had been left to itself, an island of wilderness between the two farms. Vinnie and I knew it a bit for we had hunted squirrels and such there and we had come sometimes at dusk to watch the deer drink and to listen to the bullfrogs bellow at the night but mostly we had left the spot alone for fear to rekindle the feud that had died with the ancestors. At one point, a rough shack had appeared and it was apparent that a squatter had made a third claim to the land. The woman boasted to have met the squatter once and even to have talked to him. "The old codger", the woman had called the squatter and she had spit the name. "Watch out for the old codger", she had warned.

    The shack was still there but it seemed empty that day with a hinge off the door and a board loose on the side. "Don't give the codger no never mind", Vinnie instructed, mostly to the boys who seemed timid now that they saw the shack. Vinnie scratched his head and surveyed the rock formation, struggling to find the best way to get the tree. "Ain't she a beaut", he declared enthusiastically. "She'll make a fine Christmas tree." It was a beauty ... a nice blue spruce with a straight trunk and plenty of branches to hang the ornaments. In the face of such a find, thoughts of property rights and dangers disappeared. Vinnie wandered around and around the base of the rock, stopping occasionally to look up at the tree. There really seemed no way to get at the tree except for wading through the water and then climbing the face of the cliff. Finally, he brightened. "I know how we'll get her", he said. "You just wait."

As summer turned old and began to die, we forgot the tree for a time. There was schooling to mind and the football and the harvest chores to do. But after a while the passage of the seasons was hard to ignore. The world turned gray and each day was marked by change. The geese crowded into the cut fields to fatten themselves on spilled corn for the journey south. The robins began to flock in the woods and the deer headed deeper into the forest. The squirrels, which had spent the spring and summer playfully chasing each other through the treetops, now spent their time alone on the ground, hunting acorns and hiding them in the grass. The warm west winds of summer grew bitter and cold and began to run at the house from the north. One day there was snow.

It was early December when Vinnie appeared one morning after the breakfast. He was dressed like an Eskimo for it was close to zero that day with frost on all the windows while near the barn where the creek flowed along the driveway we could see steam rising in the air as ice formed on the water. "Let's get that tree", he said ambitiously while the rest of us, full of pancakes and maple syrup, groaned and nestled further into the cushioned chairs and the woman fussed in the kitchen with the dishes. "Look", he said. "It's today or never and

Christmas is almost here." Faced with that irrefutable logic, the rest of us donned coats and scarves, gloves and galoshes and waddled out into the cold.

Vinnie had his uncle's van this time and we all piled in-Vinnie, the twins, Jeff, and me. The going was far harder than before for the snow made the hills slippery and treacherous. Vinnie was an expert driver and he managed to keep the van moving as we went uphill and to keep it from sliding on the downslopes. He had been smart enough to put snow tires on and wherever possible he avoided the snow and kept the vehicle to the places on the sun side of the hills where the snow and ice had melted, leaving only frozen ground. Still, we were only a little more than halfway to our destination when Vinnie stopped the van. "Everybody out", he commanded. "We have to walk from here." Getting out, he walked around to the back of the van, opened the rear doors, and to our surprise he extracted a long metal extension ladder. "Give me a hand here", he said. "You don't expect me to carry it, do you?"

We walked. At first, me and the boys carried the ladder, then Jeff and the boys, then me and Jeff. Vinnie led the way, keeping mostly to the road but deviating now and then when he sensed a shortcut. As we hiked along through the woods, it began to snow, a little at first and then heavier and then heavier still. Finally, the snow clouds descended on the forest like a gray shroud, floating down among the trees until their tops were obscured in the mist. We laughed and shouted to one another as we walked along and threw snowballs at each other and at the trees. After about a half hour of hiking, we reached the grotto.

We couldn't see the tree for the mist surrounded the cliff like dirty cotton. Vinnie took the ladder then and, testing the ice with his foot, he stepped tentatively onto the small pond. It held. Vinnie walked across the ice until he reached the face of the cliff and then he leaned the ladder against the rock and began to climb.

Jeff and the boys and I held the ladder firmly, looking tentatively over our shoulders at the codger's shack as we did so. We watched Vinnie disappear finally into the clouds.

After a short while, Vinnie reappeared, his expression perplexed. It seemed to us that there was something wrong. "Take a look", he said to me. Fearing that the tree had died or fallen, I climbed the ladder to see for myself. What I found both surprised and delighted me. The tree was still there, standing tall and straight . . . the perfect Christmas tree . . . but now it was bedecked with bright red ribbons, silver bows, and a star on top made from coat hangers. I stood on the ladder for a while, my head stuck into the clouds, and took it all in. Then I climbed back down. "We have to leave it", I said. "It's the codger's."

There was no disagreement. We walked back to the van. Vinnie and Jeff carried the ladder this time. The woods was quiet and mysterious and beautiful and even a bit eerie. We said little to each other, preferring the silence of the snow.

CHRISTMAS 2004

"BUTTERMILK"

My 2004 Christmas story was a failure, not because of the story itself but because of a failed experiment. As I wrote the story, I decided to insert into the story several places where I strung together various words which, I thought, should remind the readers of popular Christmas carols such as "Silent Night", "We Three Kings", and others. There are 8 places in the story where I placed the word strings. The experiment was a failure, however, because nobody (that's right, not one reader) ever came back to me and indicated they had identified the songs. Perhaps you will be able to do so.

* * *

"Buttermilk ain't come home yet", said the old man matter-of-factly as he sat to the supper. The woman shrugged and her eye rose to his but she stood silent and continued to dish the meal. I groaned. Buttermilk not home yet was trouble. A gentle animal named for the pale yellow splotch that marked her udder, that she had not followed the herd to the barn meant she was lost or, worse, hurt somewhere in the deep woods where the cows pastured by day. "You'll go", said the old man, pointing his spoon at me. I groaned again but silent this time. The milking was done and the old man would not go out again. There wasn't use to argue.

"Me too", said the Curly Head and I cringed. I hoped the old man hadn't heard but I could see he was ruminating on what she'd said. I shot the Curly Head a mean look but before I could speak the old man aimed the spoon again.

"Take her", he ordered. "She kin help". She really couldn't. She was only nine. Finding cows in the deep woods was hard work and at night harder. But it was too late. The old man had said and now he was back to the stew. The

Curly Head stuck her tongue at me. I ate the meal in silence.

Vinnie agreed to help. He arrived just as a tired sun was falling asleep on the crest of the hill behind the barn, its colored light marking the night clouds that were gathering there. We watched as they changed from pink to purple to blue like a basket of neon Easter eggs. Then we three-Vinnie, the Curly Head, and I-set out in the meadow on the path that led to the trees on the far side and eventually up the hill to the deep woods. The path was sandy and well-worn by the hooves of cows that had walked there year after year for decades. It was hot for

December and we wore only light clothes, kept warm by the effort of the climb.

It was already dark in the woods. The trees blocked the glimmer of dusk and welcomed the shadows. We listened to the night sounds as we walked-an owl screeching somewhere on our left . . . twigs crackling on our right as a raccoon or skunk shuffled in the brush . . . deer wandering among the trees. Somewhere below, in the ravine where the water collected after rain, a bullfrog began its chant.

We walked for a long distance, following the meandering of the zig-zag path until it ended in the rocks on the ridge and then we followed the ridge from hill to hill. It was the path the cows followed day after day-never deviating-as they came and went from the milking. If Buttermilk was to be found, she would be close by this path. Vinnie trudged ahead, a rope slung over his shoulder and a camping pack on his back, looking just like an eagle scout on an emergency mission.

Vinnie heard it first . . . the plaintiff bellowing from far below the ridge. It was the sound a cow makes when her milk sack is full and hurting. "Aw, geez, she's in the canyon", he said in disbelief. A cow in the canyon was bad. She might be hurt. We knew her bellowing could attract coyotes. We also knew that getting Buttermilk back up the hill would be a chore. Vinnie scratched his head in consternation.

"I'm cold", said the Curly Head just then. She stood with arms crossed and shoulders hunched. I could see she was shivering badly. The temperature was falling. Cold had come with the dark and had now begun to drift through our clothing. The colored clouds we had seen at sunset had pushed their way to us without our noticing, misting an icy rain over the top of the forest. I knew it would soon turn to snow.

"She shouldn't have come", said Vinnie. There was more worry in his voice than anger. He looked from her to me to the canyon as if trying to decide between us and the cow. "Aw, geez", he finally said and as he spoke he took his own jacket off and placed it on the Curly Head's shoulders. Taking her hand, he led her off the path to where the ridge gave way in a steep descent. I followed. Vinnie guided us a short distance down the hill, looking around and from side to side as he moved. Suddenly, he pointed to a spot where the rock had hollowed enough to form an enclosure. A tree had fallen there, its trunk positioned at the front of the hollow and its dangling limbs, still covered with leaves, resting against the rock to form a sort of natural lean-to. "There", he said. "Sit there". He took leaves from the ground and spread them on the floor of the hollow. Next, he positioned the Curly Head in the enclosure with her back to the rock and her face to the fallen tree. He quickly gathered twigs and pieces of bark and stacked them in a pile. Reaching into his pocket, he pulled out a single farmer's match, struck it on the rock, and started a small fire. "Make sure it doesn't go out", he said to me and then he was gone, moving quickly down the hill towards where we had heard the bellowing. "Aw, geez" was all he could say as he went.

It began to snow . . . a little at first with big mushy flakes and then faster and faster as the snowflakes got smaller. "Let it snow", I said to myself as I stoked the fire and held tight to the Curly Head as she lay under the coats. But then the wind fell out of the cloud and began to slap its way through the trees below, howling louder and louder as it climbed the hill towards our shelter. The snow was icy now and it began to cover the forest like crystal. It was falling sideways, biting, cutting, driven by the wind. The fire flickered and almost died. I looked at the Curly Head and saw tears in her eyes. "We'll be ok", I whispered to her but I wondered where Vinnie was.

We stayed like that for a long time-the Curly Head and I-holding each other for the warmth, tending the fire as best we could, pushing our bodies far into the hollow to avoid the blizzard's wrath. Hours passed. We slept. We woke. After a while, I just sat by the Curly Head, watching her sleep and listening to the storm. It must have been near midnight when the wind calmed and the clouds began to clear. A cushioning blanket of snow covered the woods. How still everything seemed . . . how silent! Night was closed around us like a cocoon. I felt cold. I felt warm. "I'm dreaming", I thought. I slept again.

I awoke to a commotion. Vinnie was standing over me, trying to kick sticks and leaves onto the embers of the fire and pulling with all his might on a rope. There behind him, tied to the other end of the rope and big as an elephant, was Buttermilk. I jumped to help, adrenalin flowing now to fight the frost. Getting a cow down in a barn is difficult enough but getting one to lie down in the snow is near impossible. Vinnie shouted while I pulled. Vinnie pulled while I shouted. In the end, it was the Curly Head who got the cow to lie down. "Bring her closer to the fire", she suggested and we did. Buttermilk stood there for a while as if mesmerized by the flames and then, with one soft "moo" and a swish of her tail, she lay down in the hollow. We looked to each other. Vinnie smiled. He held up his canteen and took a swig. It was milk! We all took a drink. Then we lay down against Buttermilk and, feeling the wonderful warmth of her body, we fell asleep.

Morning dawned clear and crisp. I awoke with the light. Vinnie was up already, sitting by the fire and feeding it with small pieces of bark. I lay there against the cow for a while, watching the Curly Head sleep like a baby, watching Vinnie play with the flames, listening to the sound of Buttermilk as she breathed in and out. "Hey, good morning", said Vinnie. "It's a white Christmas." He was right. I hadn't realized it but it was Christmas morning. Far away I could hear the church bells ring. I looked around and as I did, I realized something else. We were away in a manger! What a lovely day it was.

CHRISTMAS 2005

"THE CRECHE"

Death comes in many forms. There is physical death, of course, but there is also spiritual death caused by loneliness, depression, or great loss. To be alone in the midst of a crowd, to be friendless at a time of great celebration, to feel isolated from God ... all of these circumstances are forms of death. In my 2005 Christmas story I wrote about the great sadness that accompanies passages ... of life to death, of youth to age, of daylight to darkness. I also wrote about my conviction that, at the end of everything, there is still the hope of salvation and redemption and the promise of the cross.

**

It was a rainy July morning when the woman died. The old man found her when he returned from the milking. Odd he had thought of the dark empty kitchen and he had gone to the bedroom then to complain she had slept the hour and forgot the breakfast. She was lying peaceful with her head still on the pillow and hands tucked under as always. By this he knew she had passed unaware and he took comfort in it, knowing that they had grunted goodbyes in the dark before dawn.

He laid her to rest close under the maple tree near the child they had never had-the tiny miracle called only "baby boy" in the days he had been with them. The old man stood by the graves for a long time, fingering the marks on the child's stone and thinking on what monument to put on the woman's place. He looked beyond into the valley where the hills sloped gently on each side to cradle the river which gave the land its richness. Giant oaks climbed the hills toward the farm, their arms drooping low to the ground like monster apes trying to pick the wildflowers that danced there in the wind. Birds flitted in the branches and sang their varied songs. It was a good place to sleep, he thought, and then he turned away.

After, he sat by the side of the house where the woman had planted the hollyhocks and he thought on her. They had made a life here, he mused, and he looked at the briar rose which, overgrown now, filled a full corner of the yard. He remembered the day so long ago when they had laughed, he and she, as they chased the thrush from its nest there and then kissed to bless the beauty of a spring day. Hand in hand they had walked through the bluebells that carpeted the ground in the big woods, sensing the strong emotions of love. They had promised an eternity. It had not been the same, though, after the child had gone, he thought, and he wanted to weep then for a lost world but he found that the tears would not come.

He thought too about death and wondered what it was and why it was and why it had come now to take the woman and before, the child. The woman was a good woman, he thought, and nothing could be more godly and innocent than a baby. He knew, of course, what the preacher said—that it was Adam and Eve had taken the apple and brought the curse. The old man thought the apple might be a meaning for another thing but the Bible said "apple" for sure and the Bible must always be right. No matter, he thought. Death was the end of it. Ashes to ashes. Dust to dust. He closed his eyes and he was surprised at the dryness of them, as dry as the desert in his heart.

In the weeks following, the old man would mostly sit and think. There was little to do for him. He had not ever been much for talking and now he became almost mute, ignoring all those who approached him. Time and again he forgot the milking until the cows, bellowing with bloated udders, forced attention. The Mexican who tended the bees worked as best he knew and Vinnie, me and the Curly Head took the chores when we could but as the summer wore on the malaise inside the old man began to affect the very soul of the farm. Thistles and burdock invaded the grass and fought for control of the lawn. Other weeds rose tall between the rows of corn and began to strangle the plants. An uncommon and unwelcome quiet descended on the land. As summer turned to autumn, the house itself, unkept and unloved, seemed to grow old and grey, its paint peeling here and there as if it were trying to shed the skin of the very Serpent that had slithered into the world.

It was the Codger who finally brought the old man back. He was a strange one, the Codger, dressed mostly in tattered clothes with rips and tears at the elbows and knees, his long beard, bushy eyebrows and uncut hair making him always seem a wildman of sorts. His disgusting habit of chewing tobacco and spitting the chaw at whatever was close added something distinctly unfavorable to his character. The woman had always called him the "Codger" for he lived by himself in an old shack in the woods that covered the no-man's land between the old man's farm and the next. It was Vinnie had finally had the courage to talk to the man and learn that he could work wood with the skill of an artist. Vinnie had made the offer of a Christmas meal one season and each year since the Codger had returned the favor by making some holiday gift for the farm-an ornate bird house, a wooden ornament for the tree, a picture frame decorated with reindeer and rabbits, or some other trinket.

It was October when he came around the year of the woman's death, carrying with him a partially worked chunk of wood cut from the stump of a tree somewhere in the deep woods. The piece was about two feet long, narrow at one end and very broad at the other where a large, deformed lump stuck out on each side. The cuts the hermit had already made in the narrow end placed the bottom of the piece there and showed that the broad protruding end would be the top. "It'll be a crèche", the hermit announced.

Vinnie laughed at that. "You started at the wrong end", he exclaimed. "There ain't no room for the animals!"

"Everything will fit", said the Codger and he spat some chaw into the yard as if to emphasize his point. He sat the full day next to the old man, whittling on the stump. He whistled. He hummed. Once in a while he spoke but the old man did not respond. The rest of us watched and waited to see if something would emerge from the wood but we saw only indecipherable marks. Near sunset, the Codger closed his knife, picked up the stump, and disappeared into the woods without a goodbye.

It was Christmas week when he returned. By then the December wind had brought snow, piling it high in two foot drifts over the graves. The icy chill of its breath had forced the old man inside where he sat and watched in silence as Vinnie and me and the Curly Head prepared the house for Christmas. Vinnie answered the door at the knock. "It's finished", said the Codger as he stood awkwardly in the open doorway, steam rising from the cold of his coat to greet the warmth of the room. He held a burlap bag aloft as he spoke.

Vinnie ushered him in. The Codger reached into the bag and brought out the crèche, raising it high to show us all. We looked at it in astonishment. It was beautifully worked, sanded and varnished but there was no Joseph, no Mary, no cows, no sheep, no wise men, no angels. All that was there was the baby Jesus, lying in the manger, and behind, overshadowing the sleeping child was the cross. In delicate lettering beneath the manger, the Codger had cut the words of Luke 18:16: ***"Suffer the little children to come unto me, and do not hinder them, for to such belongs the Kingdom of God."*** And on the horizontal arms of the cross he had inscribed the words of John 3:16: ***"For God so loved the world that he gave his only Son, that whoever believes in Him shall not perish but have eternal life."***

The Codger moved over to the old man and handed him the crèche. The old man took it in his arms, moving his hands across the smooth wood, fingering the words again and again. He held it for a long time. He looked up at the Codger. "Thank you", he said finally. "Thank you." Then he wept.

CHRISTMAS 2006

"THE CURLY HEAD"

My Christmas story in 2006 is about a stubborn, impetuous, determined, flirty, curly-headed girl whose enthusiasm for life is infectious and thrilling. This character showed up previously in my 2004 Christmas story about Buttermilk but she plays the leading role in this story, appropriately called "The Curly Head".

* * *

"I know where Santa lives", said the Curly Head that morning at the breakfast. The farmer grunted and pretended he didn't hear while the woman ignored us from the stove where she was concentrating on the eggs. The two younger boys and I groaned. It seemed the Curly Head had been preparing for Christmas since the summer died. She had insisted that Jeff, the hired hand, bring ornaments from the basement before he went home for the winter. She had spent time at the kitchen table, creating a "toys list" for Santa and she had given it to me, instructing on postage and proper mailing technique. Now, with snow on the ground, the Curly Head was really excited and for days had been talking about nothing but Christmas. She had squealed in delight when we finally cut the tree and, with the woman's consent and to our annoyance, had stayed up late that night to burble directions on its placement and decoration. In her "I'm in charge" voice, the nine year old had even demanded the fireplace be cleaned so Santa wouldn't get his boots dirty. "I know where Santa lives", she said again.

"He lives at the North Pole", I said and the younger boys nodded. "It's far away." The Curly Head had decided that Santa lived in our woods. She had been talking about Santa's house for a week or so. At first we laughed at her. Next, we had teased her. Finally, we had become tired of it and refused to listen to her story.

"It's not the North Pole", she pouted. "It's in the woods. I sawed it." The Curly Head stuck her tongue out at me as she said it. The boys and I did the same to her.

"You 'saw' it", I corrected her. She always fell to bad grammar when she was angry. "And you couldn't have 'cause Santa doesn't let you see him until Christmas Eve."

"I did so see it. I did so", she yelled and she pounded her little fist on the table, making some of the dishes rattle. Tears welled in her eyes.

"Stop it, boys", scolded the woman as she scooped eggs from the frying pan onto the plates. She looked at me to make sure I understood that "boys" meant "boy" and she waved the pan in my direction as if to swing it at me. The farmer grunted again but he was busy eating the eggs and gave no sign the noise was directed at any of us.

"She started it", I whined but the woman swung the pan again as if it were a tennis racquet used to bounce my words back at me. I decided to keep quiet. After a while, the farmer rose, took a final gulp of coffee, and donning coat and galoshes, he walked outside without a word and strode to the barn for the milking. The boys and I followed. We had chores. The

Curly Head stood in the window and stared at us as we went.

It was afternoon when the woman came running to us. The sun, like a big orange, was already falling in the southwestern sky. The woman was upset. Her coat was open and aflutter as she ran. We could see she had not put on boots but instead, she still wore her big floppy slippers. "She's gone", the woman screamed, waiving her arms wildly. "I can't find her. She's gone."

It took a while to learn she meant the Curly Head. The Curly Head was gone. She'd searched the whole house first, recounted the woman, just to be sure of course. She'd been at the barn too but the farmer was sure the girl hadn't been there. The farmer would know, of course. Now I needed to look, urged the woman. The woman thought the Curly Head might have gone to the woods ... to look for Santa's house, the woman said. It was cold, she said. It would soon be dark. I needed to look.

I thought of Vinnie. Vinnie knew the woods like the back of his hand. He lived mostly with his uncle on the uncle's farm. It wouldn't take him long to get to us. I knew he would help. "I'll call Vinnie", I said and I walked the woman back to the house.

Vinnie arrived less than a half hour later. He was riding a horse and he had another in tow, saddled and ready. "Let's go", he said. He held the second horse as I got on and then we rode off through the meadow along the path that led to the big woods. The path was icy in spots and the snow had tried to hide it but the hooves of hundreds of cows had indented the ground over the years so that the snow pack echoed the indentations, making it easy to follow. We rode for a while in silence, listening to the snow crunch under the horses' hooves. Suddenly Vinnie shouted. "There's a track", he said, pointing to a tiny footprint in the snow. "There's another", he yelled and then he was off, urging his horse upward on the hill and into the trees.

It was darker in the forest and as night fell the trees lost all color and faded eventually to black. Only the brilliant whiteness of the snow allowed us to see. As we rode, the wind began to blow, flinging clouds of soft snow into the air in front of us and causing us to clutch our coats tightly around our bodies. I bent low and hugged the neck of the horse, feeling the animal's warmth flow against the skin of my face. We continued up the hill to the ridge, following the footprints that in turn followed the cow path. At one point, Vinnie must have realized where the tracks were leading because he pushed his horse into a trot along the path. I sped up too and we sauntered for ten minutes or so. Suddenly Vinnie pulled up. "Whoa", he said to the horse and then he put his finger to his lips to tell me to be quiet. I could smell chimney smoke and in a clearing ahead I could see a thin plume of white smoke rising from a shack where a light burned softly in the window.

My eyes got wide. I recognized the place. "It's the Codger's house", I told Vinnie. Vinnie nodded. The Codger, as the woman called him, was a hermit who lived on the disputed no-man's land between our farm and the McDuff property. The woman claimed to have seen him once. Few others had. Vinnie and I had seen the shack a year or two before when we were searching the woods for just the right Christmas tree. The Codger had not been there that time and we had never been sure that he really existed. Now, it seemed, he did.

The tracks we had been following continued straight through the clearing to the shack. Seeing this, Vinnie decided to be bold. Dismounting, he tied his horse to a sapling and then he pushed his way through the underbrush into the clearing and walked quickly to the shack. I stood behind him as he knocked on the door.

An old man opened the door. His hair was white and uncut, curling down to his shoulders. A white beard and white bushy eyebrows framed his face which was portly and marked by a reddish, bulbous nose. The man wore black, thigh-high boots and his reddish-brown suspendered pants stretched over a rather rotund stomach and slung themselves over a pinkish-red underwear shirt. "I thought you'd be coming", he said. Then he motioned us inside and pointed to a chair that had been pushed up close to an old pot belly stove which was pouring warmth into the room. The Curly Head was asleep in the chair, tucked snugly under a thick quilt. "She's asleep", said the

Codger. "She was cold and tired. I gave her some soup."

We had soup too. It was a good full-flavored broth made from pumpkin and squash and it tasted wonderful after our ride. It felt good to be out of the wind and the cold. We warmed ourselves by the fire and we talked to the Codger for a long time, admiring the cozy nest he had made inside the shack. He showed us wood carvings he had made of deer and rabbits and squirrels. Vinnie and he talked about the secret things of the forest. I told him about the Curly Head and about her excitement for Christmas. "She thought you were Santa Claus", I said to the Codger, pointing to the

Curly Head. His eyes twinkled when I said that and he put his hands on his belly and laughed.

When it came time to leave, the Curly Head was still asleep. "She can't ride", said the Codger. "You can take the sled". He led us behind the shack. To my surprise, there was an old two person bobsled there. Vinnie seemed delighted. He quickly ran around the shack to get the horses. He harnessed one, still saddled, to the sled and he tied the other to the back of the sled. Then he went back into the shack and carried out the Curly Head, still fast asleep. The Codger followed him, carrying a big pillow and several blankets. Vinnie told me to get into the sled and he sat the Curly Head next to me. The

Codger covered us both with the blankets and nestled the pillow under the girl's head. Finally, Vinnie mounted the lead horse and steered us away from the shack. I watched the Codger wave to us as we disappeared down the hill.

Christmas morning dawned a few days later. The Curly Head had hardly slept the night before and she was the first downstairs. Her whoops and hollers brought the rest of us awake and we quickly joined her by the tree. She was kneeling on the floor, three presents in front of her. There was a doll and a music box. The third present was a beautiful and intricately carved wooden sled with runners that moved. It was a bobsled just like the one we had ridden home in! In amazement, I snuck off to the front closet. I thrust my hand into the pocket of my coat and pulled out the Curly Head's letter to Santa Claus. I had never mailed it. In little girl handwriting marked out with multiple crayon colors were the words: "Dear Santa, I would like a doll and a music box and a sled."

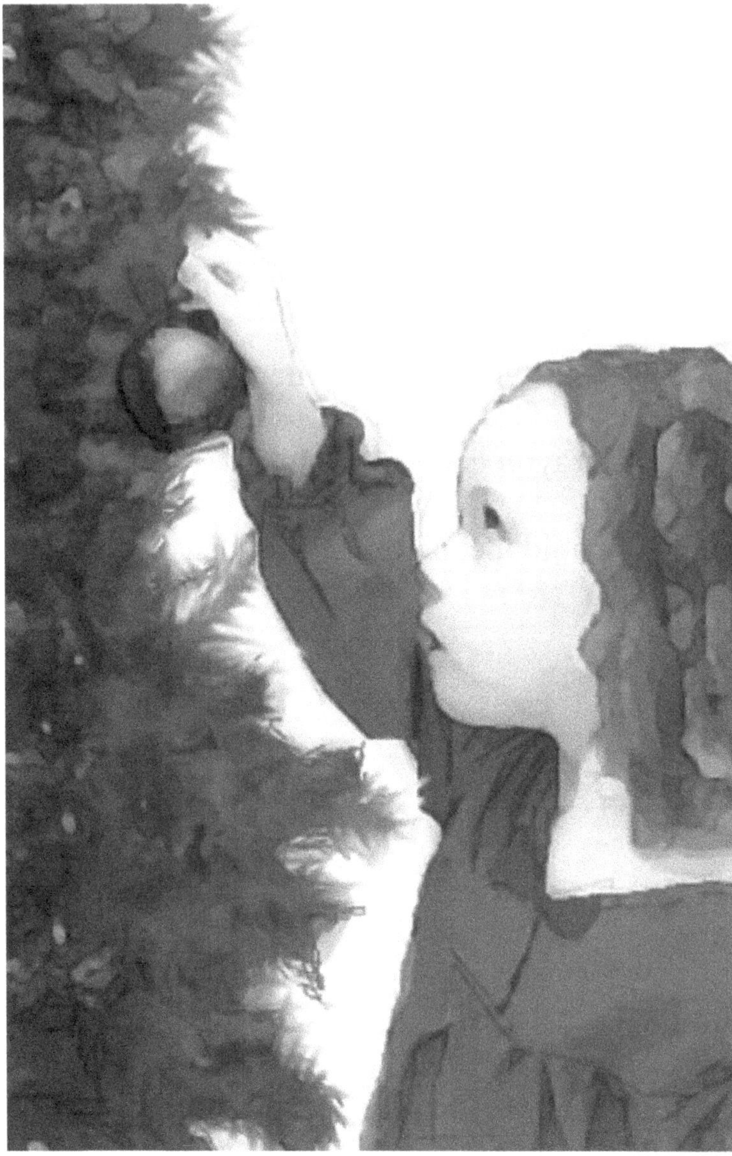

CHRISTMAS 2007

"THE PERFECT TREE"

My 2007 story was inspired by a real incident I saw many years ago. I was visiting my sister who at the time lived in a little river town called Algonquin. It was Christmas time and everyone was busily getting prepared for the holiday. One family, several houses away, had obviously wanted a BIG tree but the one they bought was so large that it would not fit through the doorway. They tried for hours but no matter what they did, no matter which way they turned or twisted the tree, they could not get it inside the house. The obvious solution would have been to shorten the tree by cutting it down to size. However, this family had a different solution. Instead of cutting the tree, they used a saw to cut into the doorway, making the opening large enough to push the tree through. I never knew what they did with the tree once they had it inside. I hoped it had a magnificent place of honor. After all, they had sacrificed a lot to get it into the house.

* * *

"It's too big", said the Curly Head. I shot her a look like as if she had two heads. So'd

Vinnie and the old man. We'd come to Felton's Field to cut a tree and we'd slogged through ankle deep snow until we'd found the perfect one, full green and good bodied. I reckoned it weren't much bigger than the old man and sure, he could've stood on a stool in the parlor spot where the woman directed to place the tree and still not touched his head to the ceiling there. I figured there were plenty of room on top for the angel the Codger had cut from the wood.

"Whata you figure, Vin?" I asked and the Curly Head pouted.

"Reckon it's fine", said Vinnie and he took the axe from the old man's truck and began to chop. "Timberrrr", he yelled when he'd finally got through and the tree fell softly in the snow, throwing a tiny crystal cloud of ice into the cold air. Vinnie bowed as if he'd just sung the lead song in a play and the old man gleefully clapped his gloved hands. I just stomped my feet to tell that I were very cold.

"It's too big", said the Curly Head again and to emphasize the words this time she sulked to the cab of the truck and closed the door behind her. She sat there, staring out the front window and refusing to look behind as Vinnie and I hoisted the tree to the bed of the truck and tied it down loose with rope, then climbed in beside and hunkered down for the frigid ride to the farm. The old man got behind the wheel and away we went.

It had snowed the night and the hills now looked as if they were covered with a thick white blanket. The valley too was a white sheet that stretched all the way to the river and beyond. The wind had already begun to push the snow here and there in sculpted drifts and where it had lingered awhile it had drawn crusty patches that now sparkled like gold and silver in the morning sunlight. It was slippery but the old man drove slowly, sliding only once or twice as he maneuvered the curves.

Wet snow clung on the trees, turning the deep woods into a watercolor of some winter scene, the dark browns of the forest brightened everywhere with patches of brilliant white. Once we saw a flash of red as a cardinal flew past against the deep green backdrop of pines and as we came near the meadow pond we saw a young buck with tiny first-year antlers chewing the low-hanging branches of a sapling. He watched us innocent and unafraid. As we rode, Vinnie began to sing "Oh Christmas Tree" and he followed with "I'm Dreaming of a White Christmas". I sang too and from the cab of the truck we could hear the old man and the Curly Head joining in. As we passed the old barn and approached the farmhouse we were well into "It's Beginning To Look A Lot Like Christmas" and our voices echoed loudly against the hills.

Jeff, the hired hand, was waiting when we arrived. He had already propped the kitchen door with one of the old metal lounge chairs and he had pushed the table aside to make a path to the parlor. We could see he had also shoveled the walk and poured salt to make an easy approach to the house from the road. The woman was fussing in the background, preparing to direct traffic.

Vinnie and I carried the tree to the door and Vinnie disappeared inside, pulling the thick bottom of the tree with him, while I pushed the top from outside. The tree went only part way and then stopped. I pushed and Vinnie pulled but the tree would not move. I could hear Vinnie grunting as he tried to drag it further into the opening and I could hear the woman, her voice rising, arguing about needles on the floor. Jeff, who had been outside with me, got down on hands and knees and crawled under the tree into the opening of the door. "It's got to turn, it's got to turn", he yelled, his bottom end still sticking out of the doorway and rising and falling as he tried valiantly to push the tree now resting on his back. For some reason, entrance from the kitchen door had always been hindered by poorly placed cabinetry, requiring a quick right and then left turn in order to enter without damage to one's head. I couldn't see but I figured it must be this causing the difficulty. The tree wouldn't budge. "Push", yelled Jeff and I pushed hard. The tree moved suddenly about a half foot and there was a crash of dishes followed by the shrill voice of the woman as she screamed something unintelligible.

"Pull it back. Pull it back", yelled Vinnie and I could still hear the woman's scolding in the background. With a mighty tug I pulled, Vinnie shoved, and the tree came tumbling out of the doorway. Jeff came tumbling out too and landed flat on his face in the snow and slush that bordered the walk. Finally, Vinnie came out, holding two of the larger bottom boughs that had broken off in the struggle. "We got to trim now", he said, pointing to the bottom of the tree that now was unevenly shaped from the loss of two limbs.

Vinnie went to the truck and came back with a saw. He began to cut at the remaining bottom branches and when he had finished that he cut off about a half foot from the stump. "It's too big", said the Curly Head. She and the old man had been standing outside on the sidewalk, watching as Vinnie, Jeff, and I shoved and pulled. Vinnie just looked at her and then scratched his head to puzzle what was next.

It was Jeff thought up the idea of the bedroom window. It was low for sure, he mused, on account of the hill being pressed there to the house and if the window'd come out, why then it'd be no trouble to put the tree through and couldn't we carry it right from there to the parlor? Vinnie seemed pleased at the idea and he grabbed the tree and began to drag it through the snow towards the back. The woman began to shout objections from the doorway but the rest of us ignored her and followed Vinnie.

The window was one of those hinged ones that swung inwards on the vertical. It looked a simple matter of just removing the storm glass, opening the window, and pushing the tree through. The opening looked big enough but Vinnie wanted to make sure so he took twine and wound it tightly on the bottom branches so the circumference of the tree was smaller.

I went inside to unlock and open the window. No sooner I'd done that than the wind rushed through the opening in search of warmth, dragging snow dust from the hill and flinging it across the bedroom. The woman saw from the parlor and screamed again. I left the window so as to calm her but just then Vinnie and Jeff began to push the tree through and just as quickly the wind grabbed the window and tried to slam it shut, pushing the stump end of the tree right through the glass. Some shard must have cut the twine then for it fell apart like the ribbon when runners hit it at the end of a race and the tightly bound branches sprung outward like a bear trap in reverse, knocking the window completely off its hinges and onto the floor. Vinnie and Jeff seemed not to notice for they continued to push the tree into the room and it fell there on top of all the bits of broken glass while I struggled with the woman and made her sit down with the promise to clean the mess.

Vinnie and Jeff carried the tree to the parlor while the woman scowled at them and nearly cried to see a trail of needles laid across the rug. The old man and I cowered in the bedroom, he nailing a plastic sheet across the window and I sweeping up the glass. The Curly Head watched in satisfaction as Vinnie cut more injured limbs from the tree and then had to shorten the stump to fit it to the tree stand. When he was finished the tree stood tall and straight and, surprisingly to me, almost touched the ceiling despite all the cutting had been done. There was just room for the treetop. I expected an "I told you so" from the Curly Head but she just smiled an impish grin.

That night we decorated the tree. The old man put on the lights and the Curly Head and I put up the ornaments. Vinnie stayed to help and it was he put on the Codger's treetop . . . a wooden angel with widespread wings. The woman watched and directed, the order of her world restored at last.

When we were done, the tree was beautiful. We stood there in the soft glow of the Christmas lights and admired it. Finally, Vinnie made some eggnog and the woman pulled out the old Victrola to play a special record with

Christmas carols. We listened to the music for a long time and it was peaceful and calming. It was as if the angels were singing directly to us. No one said anything until the Curly Head spoke her verdict. "It's a perfect tree", she said and we all agreed.

CHRISTMAS 2008

"THE CODGER"

If you look closely and compare, you will realize that my 2008 story about the Codger is, in fact, the mirror image of my 2005 Christmas story. That one was written from the perspective of the farm and the old man who had drifted into depression after the death of the woman. This one is written from the perspective of the Codger who has also suffered loss and has struggled with depression but who finds time to express faith in a way that touches the heart of the old man. The two stories, taken together, are a tale of two friends who, like wounded birds, have lost some of the ability to fly but who help each other to find a redemption that allows their souls to soar again. As you read, you will note that the Codger's faith is fragile. His situation reminds me of the man who prayed, saying "I believe. Help my disbelief".

The end of the 2008 story was intended to leave the reader with a question: Did the Codger ultimately find peace in his faith or did he not? Instead, an unfortunate typographical error left the impression that the Codger was satisfied that faith might have arrived for the old man even if it had not arrived for him. I had meant the last sentence of the 2008 story to say "For now, it was enough". The unintended change obviously altered the outcome and left me unsatisfied because faith itself, if it is stuffed with doubt, is unsatisfying.

* * *

It was still dark when he woke. From the bed he could hear the rain tattering on the window and he supposed it was the storm had startled him. He wondered about the time. The tiny cabin had no clock and the man had refused a watch since the day he'd left New York. He knew, though, that summer dawns came early to the woods and from the darkness he guessed it was still deep of night.

He lay in the bed for a time, listening to the water sounds as the storm pushed through the forest outside. Lightning threw spears of white fire into the ink of sky and the flash of them thrust into the room and pasted shadows on the wall. Thunder rolled around the cabin and shook it. The man could hear the moaning of the wind as it explored cracks in the door and tried to get inside.

The man was not afraid. He knew the cabin would last this storm as it had so many others. It was of sturdy oak and hickory planks nailed together by his very hand and all set back strong against the ridge in the no-man's land between the farms. It wasn't much, just boards set on the earth and the walls built up from there, all covered with more boards and topped with tar paper and tin. The "Codger's shack" people called it after the slander name the farm woman had given him. He didn't mind. He had been called worse in the courtrooms of the city.

Besides, the woman was gone now. Vinnie'd given the news. She'd died in her sleep, Vinnie had said, and was buried now on the hill with the child. The farmer was not good with it, Vinnie had said. He couldn't farm and he wouldn't talk. He just sat day by day as the world rusted around him. He thought on the farmer now and how he liked him-a good man who made the dandelion wine and had offered a jug for a peace gift when others had urged to chase him away and burn the shack. "I reckon ain't no one's usin' this place", he'd said, "so you might's well if you want."

    The man rose finally. The storm was moving east and the lightning had stopped, leaving only the night, but years in the cabin helped him pad his way through the black to the basin. There he splashed water on his face and let the cool of it trickle down the neck and over the shoulders. He lit a large candle and sat it to dance on the shelf where its light flickered in the mirror. As always, he saw his father's face there in his own visage, the eyes deep blue and gentle, and the familiar sadness welled in him at the thought of the man. It had been so long ago. Time was a relentless ravager, he thought-an enemy marching always onward in the singular arrow of its direction, never stopping, never turning. Time had been unkind, he thought, and had marked him with wrinkles and aged him with wide threads of white coiled in the beard and eyebrows. Some, like the Curly Head, had thought him a Santa Claus but he knew the laughter that twinkled his eyes and made his belly shake was just a mask to cover the wound.

He knew there'd be little of work today. The wet would swamp the forest floor and turn the path to mud, making the travel difficult. He'd find the raspberries, of course, and he'd tend the garden but there'd be no use to march the river path to town to barter his carvings for flour and sugar and other such. Better to stay, he thought, and work the wood.

He reached by the bed and took the chunk of oak he'd laid there. It would be a crèche, he'd told Vinnie and Vinnie had laughed at the shape, insisting there'd be no place for the animals. But Vinnie was wrong. It was his design for it to be a crèche. There'd be the baby Jesus and behind, the cross. There'd be no need for animals and shepherds and such to tell the story-only the baby and the cross. They were the story of unmatched, undeserved love, the preacher had said, and he had told how the cross, in God's plan, had always overshadowed the baby savior, foretelling the end of a journey begun in a manger.

The man wished he could believe more. "Practice faith until faith arrives", the preacher had said and he had tried to solve the mystery of that but the perfidies of the city had strangled his soul like thistles in the wheat and on the night she said goodbye the angels had cried and the leaves in the Garden withered with God's wrath. It was only then, after the Fall, that a kernel of faith had begun to grow. Perhaps one had to experience such things to build faith, he thought. After all, it is easy to believe in gods if one knows there are devils.

When he had dressed, he took the oak piece outside and sat on the bench beneath the pines. The world was already awake by then. The chipmunk that had made a home below the boards of the shack scolded his presence. Somewhere beyond the trees a meadowlark trilled its song to the dawn and close-by he heard the chatter of a chickadee. Other birds were there too-a nuthatch clinging upside down to the trunk of a tree like a crazy acrobat and bluejays screaming in the distance over some real or perceived slight. In the woods the robins were already flocking and he knew it meant an early winter. The storm was forgotten and only the slow drip-drip of water from the leaves was left to testify that it had been there.

The man loved the woods in the morning. There was something soothing there, something calming like the seashore on a sunny afternoon. He began to cut the wood, chipping and scaling unwanted parts away to reveal the image within. As he worked he listened to the forest sounds that combined into quiet poetry, as if God were whispering from the trees. This was his sanctuary, he thought. Here was salvation. Here was atonement.

The man worked the day, carefully extracting Jesus from the oak. He felt close to the baby, the carpenter's son who must also have worked the wood with his own hands. He would know, the man thought, how hard it could be, how one had to push just right with the grain to bring the colors out or how moisture could crack and warp the wood or how a blemish must be worked into the art. With each cut the man put his love in the piece, carefully shaving here and sanding there to make the wood smooth, slowly bringing out the detail that had been locked inside. It would be a fine Christmas gift for the farmer, he decided. He set the piece aside, closed his eyes, and listened to the sounds of the forest.

* * *

The wind was cold against his face as the man sloshed through the snow. The trek to the farmer's house on Christmas morning had been arduous and the ice on the ridge had made the walking treacherous. Still, the visit had been important and now, on the return to his simple shack in the no man's land, the man smiled to himself. "Thank you! Thank you!", the farmer had said-the first words he had spoken since the death of the woman-and there had been tears in his eyes as he fingered the crèche.

"Practice faith until faith arrives", the preacher had said. The man had always thought the saying was meant for him. But perhaps the crèche-his practice of faith-had let faith arrive anew in another's heart . . . the farmer's heart. It was enough.

CHRISTMAS 2009

"THE CELL"

When I wrote this story it had been almost 37 years since the end of the war in Vietnam . . . a lifetime for some and an ancient history lesson for others. I never went to Vietnam. I knew many who did. Some, including a number of young men who attended high school with me, went and did not come back. I was one of the lucky ones. Although I was drafted into the army in 1970, I was fortunate to spend my entire army time in the

United States . . . at Fort Polk, Louisiana and Fort Gordon, Georgia, and Fort Riley, Kansas. Still, that war permeated my life and the lives of many others of my generation. Night after night we watched the television as it showed the blood and the battles and the body count. We all knew young boys who were there and we shivered in fright for them and for ourselves as we realized that the world had gone mad. My son once said to me "Dad, you're lucky you never had a war." I cried at that, knowing that the war of my generation might one day be lost to history. Perhaps that is best. This story, called "The Cell", is my tribute to the war of my generation and to the many young men who fought there.

**

Vinnie sat in the dirt and watched the early sun crest the mountain, creep down into the valley, and then crawl through the bars of his cell. The morning air was heavy and the day already hot. Tropical steam rose out of the jungle surrounding the tiny hamlet, causing sweat to roll on Vinnie's forehead until it fell in great drops on his arms and legs. Some seeped into the deep wound on his thigh and the salt of it burned.

The cut was not healing. Vinnie had hoped the guards would attend it but he'd been left alone to nurse it. He'd slathered the gash with saliva, remembering how the barn cat licked its paw the night it caught on the barbed wire and how the Mexican who tended the bees on the farm and knew about natural medicines and such had commented on it and remarked there was protection in the spit. After, Vinnie had tied the wound with ragged cloth ripped from his shirt, hoping to keep it dry and clean. Now he just sat in the dust and tried to keep the leg still.

He could smell Vietnam. The sweet perfumes of jasmine and gardenia wafted up from the gardens of the villagers and mixed with the scent of banana trees, then hung briefly over the camp before colliding with the less pleasant odor of smoke, the pungent aroma of spice from the cooking fires where the soldiers prepared their breakfast, the strong smells of tobacco, coffee, and gasoline, and the putrid stench of rotting garbage, pig manure, and the black, slimy mud of the Mekong River. Vinnie had been "in country" almost a year now and he had learned that Vietnam was a land of startling contrasts that excited and frightened and ultimately overwhelmed all the senses.

    The land was lush and green as jade. At the start, Vinnie had loved the beauty and the timelessness of the place. It was as if Shangri-La, lost for centuries, had reappeared there in a vision of peace. Saigon, with its quiet parks and its colonial French flavor, seemed a calming spot of Europeanized civilization set amid verdant rice fields that stretched outward for miles and gave way finally to bucolic and changeless villages where people lived exactly as they had for centuries. But Vinnie was tired now and he knew the vision was a lie. The screams of a dozen battles plagued his sleep now and he saw that the country was drenched and sticky with blood.

    Vinnie thought on the night the platoon had been overrun. Good men had died. Others had scattered in the jungle and in the scattering Vinnie had separated. The thrust of the bayonet had brought him down in the foliage and the last thing he remembered was the hand that had reached down and stripped the tags from his neck together with the cross and its chain, a talisman gift from the Curly Head.

    Vinnie had lost track of time. It had been summer at the capture. The march to the north had taken weeks what with the constant rain, the crossing and re-crossing of the swollen rivers, and the need to hide when the choppers were overhead. Vinnie figured it must be nearing Christmas now. He thought lovingly on the farm and how it would be at the season.

The forest would be silent and covered with snow by now and the deer would be huddled in the deep woods where the warmth of the bubbling springs mellowed the winter air. In the yard, the resident pair of cardinals would be flitting back and forth between the feeder and the shelter of the spruce trees, providing a flash of red against the grey blanket of sky. At the house, the Curly Head would be preparing for the holiday and directing Jeff, the hired hand, and the younger boys where to put the furniture so as to make room for the tree. The woman would be fussing with the decorations and the old man would have retreated to the solace of the barn to reclaim the quarters where the Mexican had stayed the summer before departing on the long southward trek home. Vinnie longed to be home but he knew he would not. In the army vernacular he had been "short", with just weeks left on his tour. Now, he faced a long captivity. Sadness hit his heart and he cried.

    Later, when the sun moved beyond the bamboo cage and left him covered in shadows, Vinnie drew a Christmas tree in the dust, poking his fingertip here and there to decorate it with baubles. He drew a stickman next to the tree and topped its head with squiggles to represent the Curly Head. Then he drew another and made it wear a baseball cap just like the old man often did. The one with the full beard, like Santa Claus, was the Codger and the last figure, with a skirt and folded arms, was the woman. He tired before he could draw Jeff or the Mexican or the younger boys but for now it was enough. Vinnie looked at his creation and smiled inwardly. It made him feel better knowing that his people were with him. Vinnie closed his eyes and prayed. After a time he slept.

    The light startled him awake. One of the soldiers was in the cell, standing over Vinnie and staring intently down at the pictures on the ground. The soldier's right hand waived a revolver vaguely in Vinnie's direction while the other held a torch low over the dust drawings. Vinnie cowered instinctively, fearing the power resting in the weapon . . . knowing already the cruelty of the guards. Vinnie felt like a schoolboy caught doodling in class or worse, like the spy whose hidden message had been discovered in the microdot. In either case, swift punishment could be the result.

As Vinnie watched, the soldier slowly raised his booted foot and moved it over the lines on the ground. Vinnie expected the boot to come crashing down to obliterate his crude work. But it didn't. The soldier's foot came down softly at a spot just above the top of the Christmas tree. The soldier dug the tip of his boot into the soft dirt and dragged it downward, forming a vertical line. Then he struck a horizontal line running straight through the vertical mark. Vinnie stared in amazement at what the soldier had made. It was a cross! It was a cross that now stood proudly atop the Christmas tree!

The soldier looked at Vinnie. He lowered the revolver and placed it back into the holster on his hip. Then he reached into his pocket, pulled something out, and handed it to Vinnie. It was the talisman cross that had been taken from Vinnie at his capture. After a moment, the soldier walked around Vinnie and began to leave the cage. When he got to the door, he stopped and turned. He nodded once at Vinnie and then he disappeared into the night, leaving the door unlocked and ajar.

Vinnie was wide awake now. He blinked and tried to comprehend what had happened. Like one of the biblical angels in the miracle stories he had learned at the Sunday school, a soldier in the North Vietnamese army . . . a Christian soldier . . . had just delivered him. He could scarcely believe it. Vinnie fingered the talisman cross the soldier had returned. He could feel the etching the Curly Head had taken from the 46th Psalm and inscribed there when he had left for the army:

"Come, behold the works of the Lord, how he has brought desolations on the earth. He makes wars cease to the end of the earth. He breaks the bow and shatters the spear. He burns the chariots with fire. "Be still and know that I am God...."

In the dark, Vinnie slipped from the cage and drifted into the jungle. He knew that he was going home.

CHRISTMAS 2010

"SANTA'S MOONWALK"

I always remember the practical jokes my uncle and the others who worked on the farm liked to play on one another. Most were hilariously funny like the time my Aunt Clara rigged the pinochle deck and secretly substituted it for the real one so my uncle unwittingly dealt everyone at the table a double run, leading to some outrageous bidding and lots of intemperate words when the scheme was finally uncovered. Another time, a friend and I spent the wee hours of the morning in the hen house, removing all the real eggs and replacing them with golf balls so my aunt was totally confused when she later came to collect for the breakfast. Sometimes the jokes went awry. This year's story is about one such episode.

* * *

It was Jeff's idea. Jeff, the hired hand, was normally docile, not wishing to offend, I suppose, and perhaps not quite confident in his thoughts. That he spoke at all was mostly a miracle of sorts. "The tall, quiet type" was what the girls giggled in their groups whenever he came to town for the buying at McGinty's general store. Even the Curly Head loved him in her childish-crush way and Jeff adored her, of course, as if she was his little sister.

It was this affection, I think, made him decide to put the idea into practice. He would certainly need rope, he knew, and lots of cardboard, the all of which could be gathered in the barn. He would need a ladder too so's to climb the monster oak tree that stood tall in the back yard overlooking the valley. And he would need help. That's where Vinnie and I came in.

It was simple, he explained. The paper had said it were to be a blue moon on Christmas

Eve, the second full of the month. He had seen how the moon always rose right where the oak stood and how when the owls and nighthawks fled the tree at dark they were outlined against the face of it. Well, what if Santa Claus could fly from the tree and be silhouetted too? Wouldn't that be a funny surprise for the Curly Head? After all, she were always on about Santa and writing him notes and setting out milk and cookies and such. Couldn't some preparation and ingenuity make it happen? Vinnie and I laughed at the thought and quickly joined the scheme.

The next week was spent in the barn, painting Santa's sleigh and eight tiny reindeer on a large cardboard sheet and carefully extracting them with knife and scissors. Vinnie poked holes at the top and strung heavy twine through, tying the ends in a loop. Then he attached the loop to a length of heavy rope.

    After, Jeff dragged the ladder from the basement and set it for the ready against the tree. Carrying the cardboard with the rope trailing behind, Jeff climbed the tree and placed the cutout just right, hiding it deftly in the dry leaves that still clung there against the wind and making it look nothing more than a squirrel's nest. Next, he strung the rope along one of the branches that stretched towards the back porch, dropping the end finally so it hung down and hugged the house along the drain pipe. From the rocking chair where he sat, Vinnie could just reach it.

On Christmas Eve, everything was ready. The almanac recorded when the moon would appear so we took places a half hour before. Jeff, bundled warmly in his red parka, climbed the tree once more and got ready to drop Santa's sleigh while Vinnie and I took our places on the porch. Then we waited.

Right on time the moon rose big and orange like a giant balloon. It rested briefly on the crest of a hill across the valley and then it began to rise slowly, deflating as it went and turning white like a frozen snowball. Vinnie watched closely as it approached the appointed branch and as it got there he whistled sharply. At the signal, Jeff dropped the cardboard from the tree and then Vinnie began to pull wildly on the rope, making the sleigh and reindeer dip and bob. "Santa, Santa", I screamed as I had been instructed and I opened the door and stuck my head in to make sure the Curly Head could hear. "Santa, Santa", I screamed again.

    The Curly Head came running out in time to see Santa's sleigh dancing on the face of the moon and her eyes widened in wonder at the sight. What we hadn't counted on, however, was the curiosity of the others who had not been told of the plot. Seconds after my shout brought the Curly Head, the door burst open again and the old man shot out onto the porch, followed by the woman and the younger boys. Their suddenness startled Vinnie and he dropped the rope which then slid back along the branch.

With the tautness gone and the rope snaking towards Jeff, the sleigh began to dive towards the ground. Jeff, in a desperate attempt to catch it, lost his hold on the tree and fell in a tumble across the light of the moon, the red of his coat splashing by in a flailing flash of color.

"Santa", exclaimed the Curly Head excitedly and she stomped her foot in delight and pointed at Jeff crossing the moon. The rest of us watched in horror as Santa, his sleigh and his reindeer somersaulted down and disappeared into the tangle of the brier rose bush that spread out below the tree and down the hill to the valley.

The Curly Head slept soundly that night, safe in the assurance that she had seen Santa Claus. At the morning, the presents were all there and the milk and cookies were gone, proof that Santa had survived the fall. Jeff was there too, scratched and sore but otherwise intact... and very happy.

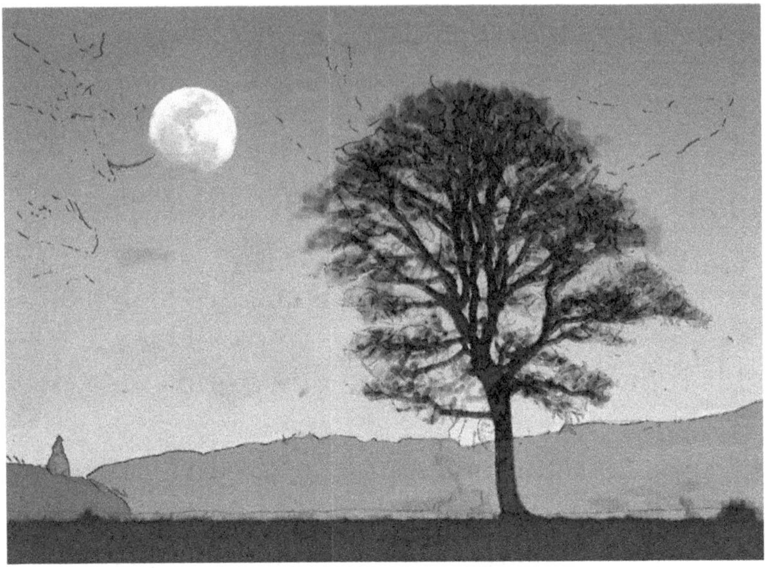

CHRISTMAS 2011

"THE RUDE ELF"

For children, Christmas tradition is one of the things that makes the season so wonderfully, delightfully, fantastically, miraculously beautiful. The sights, the sounds, the smells, the lights, the music ... it is the mix of these that adds magic to the world and produces memories that lead so many people back home each winter to celebrate the birth of the Baby. And what an enormous celebration it is, filled with significance and promise everywhere! While I do not want the secular to overpower the sacred, I also do not want the sacred to banish the secular. I believe with all my heart that God sends us such beauty at Christmastime so that we might laugh and sing along with the angels who proclaim the arrival of the Savior. This year's story is about one family experiencing all the magic of Christmas.

* * *

No sooner the harvest was in with the corn and soybeans cut and the fields plowed than the farm, sensing the tasks were over, began to settle to winter's sleep. One by one the days ran short and the sun turned distant as it rolled on the southern ridge before plunging each afternoon into the deep woods where the darkness lived. It was the dull season when summer's mirth lay frozen in the lawn and autumn's crisp beauty was faded and blown away with November winds. Only the somber browns of the oaks lingered on branches that waved like bony fingers over the barren land.

It was the snow brought life back to the place. One night the rains came and pelted the house. The cold followed and by morning the sodden earth had hardened and turned to ice and a thick white sheet was thrown on the ground, entombing the last of the roses and piling in a great wrinkled mass against the barn.

The twins were first to notice. Up at dawn with the farmer, they had raced to the window to poke at the pictures left by Jack Frost. "It snowed", they screamed in wonder as they pranced through the house, waking everyone in their excitement and forcing the farmer to take his coffee and trudge early to the milking.

    We all knew the change in weather signaled the great celebration had begun and in the days following we eagerly fell to new chores required in the preparation. Jeff, the hired hand, got the Christmas boxes from the basement while the farmer strung the outside lights and Vinnie and I trekked through drifts to the far end of the meadow to cut the tree we had selected months before. The woman set out candles and she got down the stash of records with the holiday music, picking her favorite, Silent Night, to play its scratchy tune throughout the house. Good cheer was everywhere and even the farmer could be heard whistling as he worked. This year there was to be a Christmas parade in the town and the thought of it made everything doubly festive.

    It was only the Curly Head wasn't happy. She'd been to the Codger's shack in the no-man's land between the farms where she believed Santa Claus lived and she'd returned in a pout. "Santa won't come now", she exclaimed and she stared at me through teary eyes.

"He always comes", I said distractedly. I was busy putting together a model airplane with glue and sticks and such and I didn't want to be involved in the Curly Head's trouble.

"He won't come", she insisted and she stomped her foot and started to cry. "He gots a new elf what's rude and he don't help Santa fix his sleigh so Santa can't come. He's a poor elf what makes him mean and nobody likes him." She was shouting now and pointing her finger at me as if I had done something wrong.

I wanted to correct her grammar but I didn't say anything. I just shook my head and wondered where she came up with this stuff.

My silence seemed to upset her even more and she stalked off towards her room. After the Curly Head left, the woman poked her head in from the kitchen and seemed about to say something but she kept quiet when she saw me innocently patching the sticks together.

The Curly Head's mood didn't change in the days leading to Christmas. Instead, she became more sullen and refused to help in the decorating. She kept to her room and she cried a lot. No persuasion could convince her that Santa Claus would still deliver toys on Christmas Eve like always. "He gots a rude elf" was all she would say.

It was Vinnie decided we should ask the Codger what had been said to the Curly Head. She was certain the Codger was Santa Claus and, truth be told, he looked like Santa Claus with his white hair, flowing white beard, and his big belly. We thought he must like the comparison because he sometimes enhanced the thought by wearing red pantaloons supported with wide red suspenders. No matter. We needed to discover what had happened to make the Curly Head so sad. Thus it was we set out on horseback that Saturday morning, a week before the big parade, to visit the Codger.

He was in the yard chopping wood when we got there. No one in the area seemed to know how old the Codger was but that morning he seemed as vigorous as any, his muscled arms wielding the axe above his head as if it were a wizard's wand. He plowed it hard into the wood once he saw us and it stuck there like Arthur's sword, waiting for someone strong enough to remove it. "Ho ho! Merry Christmas", he shouted his greeting as we approached. As the words bounced through the forest, he put his hands on his belly, leaned back, and laughed.

Vinnie and I liked the man. People had feared him at first, thinking him a wild man of sorts when he had suddenly appeared in the woods, and the woman had given him the slander name that had stuck. Everyone called him the Codger now and his real name was forgotten. Vinnie and I considered him a friend. That morning he took us in to his cozy shack and we sat by the fireplace and explained about the Curly Head. He listened intently but when we had finished he reached for a book that had been lying on the table. He looked at us with a twinkle in his eye and, opening the book, he poked a fat finger at some of the pictures there. We laughed when he showed us and suddenly everything was very clear. He reached over with his hand and drew us close. "Here's what we can do", he whispered with a conspiratorial tone.

The next Saturday we all left early for the town, anxious to see the Christmas parade. The day was beautifully bright and only modestly cold. There had been more snow and now the fence posts and lamp stands all sported small mounds that looked like fluffy little pillows while large drifts sculpted by the winds lined the roads where people from the town mingled gaily with the country folk. A loudspeaker blared Christmas music and members of one of the churches passed through the crowd handing out hot chocolate, apple cider, and doughnuts.

Each of us was in the spirit except tor the Curly Head who still moped over the elf.

    The parade started promptly at noon, led by the mayor and his wife who were bundled in coats and scarves, mittens and muffs and who rode incongruously in the back of an open convertible on such a winter's day. The high school marching band came next and was followed by a float put together by the 4-H club. Fire trucks were next, all festooned with green, silver, and red ribbons. Then came various cars with signs touting the town's businesses, schools, and churches. As watchers we all waved and shouted but the Curly Head still refused to participate. She just stood silent and watched as if it was a funeral procession instead of a parade.

Suddenly the loudspeaker began to play Here Comes Santa Claus and a murmur rushed through the crowd as people pushed forward for a view. "Santa", came the shout from a hundred and more voices. "Santa! Santa!" Simultaneously, Vinnie bent down and swooped up the Curly Head up onto his shoulders so she could see that the focus of the crowd was a ruby-colored four seat bobsled. Standing in the sled waving to the crowd was the Codger, dressed now in an authentic Santa suit with black boots, wide black belt, and a red suit and hat with ermine fur. The sled was pulled by eight magnificent horses, each camouflaged with an antler headdress to mimic a reindeer and in front of them was Buttermilk, our cow, also crowned with antlers and fastened with a huge red ball on her nose.

As we watched in amazement, the music changed to Rudolph the Red-Nosed Reindeer. Santa stopped the sled right in front of us. He held up a book, opened it, and he began to speak as he thumbed the pages and pointed at pictures. You see, he said, a drowsy little girl had fallen asleep as he read a story and she had gotten it wrong. There was no rude elf but rather, Rudolph, a reindeer. Rudolph wasn't mean and he was only poor because the other reindeer didn't understand him and, not understanding, they wouldn't play with him. And yes, Santa needed Rudolph to make his sleigh work. But the little girl, having fallen asleep, missed the best part of the story. Rudolph helped Santa guide his sleigh that frightfully foggy night and then all the other reindeer loved him. Because of this, Santa assured the crowd, there certainly would be a Christmas.

We watched the face of the Curly Head as Santa spoke. At last, she was smiling.

CHRISTMAS 2012

"THE POSTCARD"

There was rain. The young woman had known it would come for morning winds had pushed fog from the ocean and had banished the sun by midday, leaving only ominous grey clouds to threaten the city. Now, as dusk approached and blackness began to descend, the storm grew angry and poured its rage in torrents against the window, pressing a dreariness into the apartment where the woman stood.

The woman put her nose on the glass and watched as the world turned dark. Far below, the after work crowd was scurrying along Broadway toward Times Square and the trains beyond, umbrella battling umbrella for space. Snarls of evening traffic were snaking slowly over the George Washington Bridge, red taillights painting lines in the night. On the streets below she could vaguely hear the blaring of car horns as driver fought driver.

She was not prepared for Christmas, she knew. Unusual warmth had forced the crowds outside to chase a dream of perpetual summer and seasonal displays had been ignored as the holiday approached, causing merchants to fret about profits and losses. Even her flat was not ready. She looked now across the room at the scrawny tree, only half decorated, and at the desk where unwritten cards lay strewn among bits of ribbon and wrapping paper. Behind, on the wall, the clock marked time with a tsk tsk tsk disapproval at the passage of another day wasted in busyness.

The woman sat back in the window nook and rested her head against the pane. She closed her eyes for a long time and just listened to the wind roaring outside. The melancholy rhythm of the water sounds made her feel as if the whole world was covered with tears. Friends would imagine that she was happy, she knew. After all, to sing and dance in the theaters of New York . . . to be applauded by adoring audiences everywhere . . ., well, that really was something they would say . . . that was a dream come true they would say. But she knew better now. Her soul was empty now and she was tired.

She reached in her pocket and retrieved the card that had arrived in the post. The front was a picture of a cute curly-headed girl holding a candle in a darkened room. The back was just inked words with no signature but she knew from the writing it was from him and this had surprised her. There had been news from Howard only once before since he left the city and that soon after he'd gone. She'd been glad at that first word, of course, and had laughed when he told of the shack in the woods and how people called him "the Codger" and how he had befriended the farmer and a nice young man named Vinnie. But there had been silence since then and the months had grown long.

She thought on him now, remembering a rustic road they had taken that last summer day when they had escaped New York to explore the countryside. She remembered the carpets of butterflies resting on sun-dappled pavement and how Howard had marveled and laughed when they ascended in a great colored cloud as the car approached. That was also the day he had said he was leaving and he had asked her to come with him. His soul was being strangled, he had said. He needed a simpler life . . . a simpler place, he had said, where the voice of God was not drowned out by the cacophony of the city. Come with, he had said. But she had demurred. The Great White Way was calling and fame was beckoning with bejeweled fingers, a Faustian bargain set before her innocence. If only she had known, she thought. If only she had known.

    The woman knelt then and prayed the prayers she had been taught as a child in the Sunday School. When she had finished she lowered her head against her chest and wept as great waves of sorrow washed over her. After the sobs had subsided, she looked again at the card. The Curly Head smiled on the front and the candle shone brightly in the dark. The woman turned the card over then and re-read the words penned there. "Come home", they said simply, and below was the Bible verse from John 1:5. **The light shines in the darkness and the darkness has not overcome it.** There was peace in the words and suddenly a calmness entered the room. She looked out the window again and realized that the rain had turned now to snow. It was then that she made her decision. She was going home for Christmas.

THE END